The Pure World Comes

Rami Ungar

To Jennifer,
Happy reading and
pleasant nightmares
~ Rami Ungar

Published by Rami Ungar, 2022.

THE PURE WORLD COMES

First edition. May 10, 2022.

ISBN: 978-1393985549

Written by Rami Ungar.

This book is dedicated to Kaoru Mori. Without her manga *Emma*, my love of the Victorian era, and this book, would not be possible.

The Good therefore may be said to be the source not only of the intelligibility of the objects of knowledge, but also of their existence and reality; yet it is not itself identical with reality, but is beyond reality, and superior to it in dignity and power.

—Plato, *The Republic*, Book VI

Jack. You're quite perfect, Miss Fairfax.

Gwendolen. Oh! I hope I am not that. It would leave no room for developments, and I intend to develop in many directions.

Oscar Wilde, *The Importance of Being Earnest*, Act I

Chapter One

Spring, 1894

London, England

A stream of shit and piss fell from the second floor of the Avondale house to the street below, where it mixed with the piss, shit and mud that already littered the avenue. From the second-floor window of Mr. Avondale's dressing room, Shirley Dobbins put down the chamber pot belonging to Mr. and Mrs. Avondale and picked up the one belonging to their daughter, Miss Lucinda. A pungent odor wafted out as she removed the lid. Shirley wrinkled her nose and quickly dumped the contents into the street.

Now that's how you get it done, she thought with a sense of satisfaction. Closing the window and replacing the lids on the pots, she peeked out the door to make sure the coast was clear before rushing along the hall and down the stairs with the pots tucked under her arms. Her employer, Mrs. Avondale, would be mortified if she knew one of her maids threw her family's nightsoil out her husband's dressing room window. However, she also wanted her maids to empty, wash and replace the pots quicker than either maid could manage. Going that pace threatened to spill nightsoil onto the carpet and Shirley didn't even want to consider the consequences of such an occurrence.

Hence, she and Nellie dumped the nightsoil out the windows in the morning, a practice common amongst homes not fitted with the new flushing toilets she had heard about. And why not? Doing so was efficient and allowed more time for other tasks.

As she passed by the parlor, Shirley slowed her pace to an unobtrusive amble. Among other things, Mrs. Avondale disliked her maids walking by the parlor too fast while she was in there. Even if those maids were holding chamber pots under their arms and needed to wash them out as soon as possible. Thus, Shirley always had to slow down until she was well past the room.

2

When she thought she had gone far enough, Shirley quickened her pace. No screech from Mrs. Avondale or stomp of shoes followed after her, filling the young maid with relief. Down another flight of stairs, through the kitchen and Shirley entered the scullery. Nellie Dean, the other maid-of-all-work, was elbows-deep in scrubbing the dishes from breakfast and was going much too slow about it.

"Nellie, let me take over," said Shirley. She did not wait for the younger girl to move, but instead pulled a plate out of Nellie's hand and started scrubbing. "Look, this is how you hold the brush. See? Scrubbing like this gets everything off faster."

Nellie suddenly became very interested in her feet. "I-I'm sorry," she murmured.

Shirley ignored the apology. Apologies and forgiveness took up valuable chore time. "Go wash out the chamber pots and take them back upstairs. And remember what I told you about going past the parlor when the missus is in there."

Nellie nodded, picked up the pots, and hurried into the back yard. As soon as she was gone, Shirley heaved a sigh. She had not meant to be short with the girl. She was only twelve and this was her first position serving a family. She was still learning how to do all the chores required for the upkeep of a home, as well as attend to the needs of her employers. Shirley, on the other hand, had begun working when she was ten and had served in two homes prior to the Avondales. After six years as a maid, she should know better than to get annoyed with Nellie, who looked up to her both as a mentor and as an older sister of sorts.

But even with two maids, there was much to do in this house. Too much, if Shirley was honest with herself. While not a mansion, the house had more rooms than those owned by families of comparable class to the Avondales. And the Avondales, wishing to impress all who visited with their wealth and status, made sure no room went unused.

And all those rooms, with their furniture and knickknacks and whatnot, had to be cleaned at least once a week. And that was in addition to emptying the fireplaces, buying food and preparing meals, sweeping the front stoop, polishing the banisters, washing the windows, and, on Mondays, collecting and washing the laundry. Which, even with the help of a local washerwoman who came by on Mondays to assist, could take a whole day to complete.

This, and several dozen more tasks, had to be completed every day. And every day, Shirley and Nellie had to complete them while also factoring in time to change their uniforms, caps and aprons for each task. And they had to change in a small closet by the entrance to the back yard at least three to four times a day without poking each other's' eyeballs out with their elbows, because the Avondales didn't have servants' quarters on the top floor.

It was no surprise that, by the time all those chores were completed, both maids would collapse in front of the oven in the kitchen and doze right off. After all, without a servants' quarters, they needed a warm place to sleep, and the kitchen was warm. Sometimes they were too tired to even remove the cockroaches they crushed as they fell. And there were always cockroaches under them as they fell.

Of course, the burden of maintaining this house would be greatly alleviated if Mrs. Avondale or Miss Lucinda helped. In most homes, the mistress and her daughters usually assisted the servants with the workload in some capacity if simply hiring more servants was not an option. Shirley would have been thrilled if her mistresses deigned to help her. Work would not be so exhausting and she would have more time to tutor Nellie in the finer points of housekeeping.

Unfortunately, the Avondales were aspiring to a higher class than they currently occupied. Thus, it was unthinkable for Mrs. Avondale, the wife of the founder of a successful drill and corkscrew manufacturer, or her daughter, who would probably marry a fine gentleman, or even a baron's son, to do housework! After all, what would the neighbors say?

If Sarah Fagan, the previous maid who had served alongside Shirley, had still been working, it would not be so bad. Sarah had been experienced, and Shirley had worked well with her. But Sarah, dear woman, had retired to her daughter's in Suffolk for her health, technically making Shirley the head maid of the house. And with a younger maid to train, it often felt like Shirley was the only one doing any of the work.

Well, at least the Avondale's son, Griffin, was away at Eton. Shirley had to be grateful for that. If she had to deal with him and his antics on top of everything else, she might scream.

She heaved another sigh as she wiped the last of the pans dry and hung them in the cabinet. *Just fight through it*, she reminded herself. *One day, you'll be the head housekeeper of a large manor, with a large and well-trained staff working under you, and you can use this story to show the new maids how one rises to the same position as you.*

Her stomach rumbled then. She was hungry. Breakfast was not something indulged in by women of her profession. Instead, they ate bites of whatever leftovers from the family's breakfast were available and made do on that. Shirley left the scullery to see what was available, and instead found Lucinda Avondale stuffing the last rasher of bacon into her mouth. She caught Shirley's look of surprise, smirked, and made satisfied chewing noises.

"Absolutely delicious," she said, her Queen's English as distinct from Shirley's London cockney as day was to night. "You know, I thought I had my fill at breakfast. But that bacon you and the other girl prepared was so tasty, I just had to have more."

Shirley's anger flared. Not for the first time, she wanted to give this pampered young woman a good kick in the backside. However, she managed to keep her temper in check and cleared her throat. "Is there something I can do for you, Miss Lucinda?"

"Oh, I am content," Lucinda replied, laughing in that loud, contemptuous way she had. "Seeing that ugly face of yours was pleasure enough! Oh, but you and Billie or whatever her name is should pick up the pace. Mother is becoming rather annoyed that the beds have not been made yet."

"Nellie and I will take care of it now," Shirley replied as the younger girl returned from placing the chamber pots upstairs again. "Right, Nellie?"

The younger girl was confused, as would anyone upon walking in midway through a conversation, but nodded her head and uttered a quiet "Yes, miss," anyway.

With a loud *hmph!* Lucinda swept past Nellie and back into the hallway, probably to the drawing room to work on her sewing. Pushing her temper deep down so she would not have to deal with it, Shirley grabbed Nellie by the wrist and pulled her upstairs again.

That was a low blow, she thought, remembering how Lucinda had snatched up the last shred of bacon. *Wanted more, my foot! And does she always have to bring my looks into it?*

Shirley was well aware she was far from the most beautiful young woman in London. While her brown hair was unremarkable and her face alone was far from horrible, she had a lazy eye that was always looking out to the side. And while her vision still worked well enough for her to clean, cook, read and write, that one eye tended to offend and horrify some people. In fact, whenever the Avondales held dinner parties, she was often relegated to the kitchen while Nellie and a servant hired for an evening's work waited on the guests so as not to upset them.

Lucinda, however, had a perfect face and eyes, which she loved to brag about in front of Shirley whenever she got the chance. And while the obnoxious brat had red hair, a color most certainly out of fashion with high society, it was more of a wine-red than an orange-red.

In some lights, it even looked black, which instantly made her more desirable.

With her looks, along with being the daughter of the president of a drill company, it would not be unreasonable to expect Lucinda to marry into the upper classes, or maybe into the peerage! Because of these factors and Shirley's position relative to Lucinda, the young woman believed with all her heart that it was not only her privilege to constantly mock Shirley, but her right.

Hard to believe she's only a year younger than me, Shirley thought, *the way she acts. I wonder if she uses those same manners when suitors come to call.* She allowed herself a private smirk. *Well, even if she manages to get a husband, I'm certain he'll be upset when he realizes how much nightsoil she passes most nights.*

***

Somehow, despite how the morning had gotten away from them, both maids managed to complete their morning chores in time to serve Mrs. Avondale and Lucinda a light luncheon in the dining room. As Shirley placed a platter of cold pheasant from last night in the center of the table, she checked Mrs. Avondale's expression. Her employer ignored her, focused entirely on studying and making notations on a piece of paper in front of her. Good. When Mrs. Avondale paid attention to her at lunch time other than to ask for seconds, it was usually because she was displeased with something her maid had done.

Nellie set down a bowl of greens and stepped back. Like clockwork, Shirley stepped forward to pour the ladies some water.

"Shirley," said Mrs. Avondale, still perusing her paper.

Shirley stiffened. Just her name. No request for a certain food or anything else related to the meal. Either Mrs. Avondale had a task for her, or Shirley was about to be punished for something she did wrong. And experience had taught her that it was usually the latter.

Gulping, she turned towards her employer. "Yes, ma'am?"

For a minute, her mistress did not reply, instead taking some cuts of pheasant and placing them on her plate. Then Mrs. Avondale thrust the paper she had been writing on a moment ago at Shirley. "Mr. Avondale and I are hosting the Martins tomorrow evening. I want you to go to the market after luncheon. Purchase everything on this list. I will give you the funds for it all before you go. Do not leave a single thing out." She placed extra emphasis on the last sentence.

While she kept her face impassive, Shirley exhaled with relief as she took the page, which turned out to be a menu. "Yes, ma'am. Thank you, ma'am."

She examined the menu. Mock turtle soup, venison, lobster, pheasant—goodness, the Avondales did enjoy their pheasant, didn't they? Ice cream for dessert. Various wines, sherry, and coffee. This would be a rather exorbitant dinner party. She would need to consult Sarah's recipe book in the kitchen before going out to be certain, as well as what was in the pantry, but she had a fairly good idea of what she would need and which shops she would have to visit.

Having assigned Shirley her task, Mrs. Avondale turned her attention to a slice of pheasant. "I will be heading out after luncheon to visit Mrs. Simon. My husband will be accompanying me there, so there is no need to call a carriage. Is that understood?"

"Yes ma'am," said Shirley.

"Yes ma'am," said Nellie.

"I will not be gone long. When I get back, I expect tea to be ready."

"Yes ma'am."

"Yes ma'am."

Her orders given, Mrs. Avondale finally began eating, conversing with her daughter in-between bites on the latest gossip in their social circles and plans for an upcoming trip to Germany the family were to take next year, should Mr. Avondale's business continue to do well. Shirley and Nellie took their opportunity to step out and get started on the afternoon chores, returning to the dining room every few minutes to refresh Mrs. Avondale's and Lucinda's glasses and see if they needed anything else.

Finally, with luncheon done and the plates in the scullery for cleaning, Shirley consulted Sarah's recipe book before entering the closet to change. With her apron hung up and her coat slung over her arm, she left the closet and dipped into the scullery. Nellie was already washing the dishes and was doing it the correct way this time.

"Excellent work," she said, stepping beside Nellie. The younger girl jumped and turned to Shirley with startled eyes.

"O-Oh! Thank you," she said nervously.

"You remember what's for supper tonight?"

Nellie nodded, a glint of confidence in her eyes. "Cockles and lamb, with boiled and seasoned potatoes. I'll get started on them as soon as I've finished with the tea."

Shirley smiled. Nellie may have been inexperienced when it came to maintaining a house, but she was born for cooking. No matter the dish, the ingredients or the preparation involved, she took them all in stride and cooked them to perfection, even if she had never seen the recipe before. Shirley had no doubt that, one day, Nellie would be the head chef of a large household. Perhaps even a noble family if life was kind to her.

Though I won't tell her that, she thought as she went to find her employer. *It won't do to give Nellie too big a head at that age.*

After receiving the funds to purchase the ingredients for tomorrow's dinner and a lecture on what should happen should she come home without even one item, Shirley went out the back door in the kitchen and into the back yard. She then strolled around to the front of the house and then took off in the direction of the Underground. This was another requirement for working for Mrs. Avondale: family members and guests used the front door. Servants and handymen used the back door. Shirley had no idea if this was some oddity of Mrs. Avondale's, as the last two homes she'd worked for had not cared which door she'd used, but she didn't care enough to ask. Or was it that she was too wary of punishment to ask?

As she made her way down the block, she heard horses' hooves and glanced behind her. A hansom cab had stopped in front of the Avondale house and a man in a suit had stepped out. It was Mr. Avondale, right on time to escort his wife to her friends' home and then go about whatever business he had. Paying it no further mind, Shirley headed off, unaware of the significance of that last glimpse of her employer's husband.

***

Things were certainly noisier than usual when she arrived at Covent Garden, which in Shirley's opinion, had the finest produce and meats in all of London for the best price. It was also fun to walk through: up until about sixty years ago, Covent Garden had been a sprawling open-air market filling up all the streets and creating crowded and unsanitary conditions. To help alleviate this issue, the market was reorganized in a brick-and-glass building. While this had helped for a while, the market had continued to grow, and was now back to spilling out onto the surrounding streets.

Shirley visited here as often as she could for groceries, and when she did, she liked to look around at the many shoppers, the stalls hawking everything from food to clothes to tea sets and even a variety of exotic animals, and imagine the consternation of the politicians who had hoped their big building had forever rid the city of this disorganized market.

Today though, something seemed different. Crowds at Covent Garden were nothing new. In fact, it was the crowds that kept the market growing and continued to cause traffic problems. But today it seemed even more crowded, especially by one of the entrances to the building. Shirley approached, and saw that everyone had gathered around a raised platform in which a man with a pointy beard, a bright red coat and a top hat was speaking to the crowd. Some sort of performance was occurring.

"Now, watch closely, ladies and gentlemen, boys and girls!" the entertainer called with an American accent. Beside him on a table was a clear glass tube about a meter tall and rounded at the top. The entertainer picked up the tube and showed it to the audience, revealing the bottom end of it was attached to a pump. "This process is how they create the lightbulbs Mr. Edison produces in America! You see, they burn out quickly if oxygen is within the bulb! Oxygen, as you might well know, is what is in the very air we breathe! But remove it, and the bulb will glow bright enough to keep your streets lit at night for over a year. Observe!"

The entertainer began to pump, explaining what he was doing over the loud sucking noise the instrument made. "I will draw out the oxygen from this tube. I will then disengage the tube from the pump." He did as promised, being careful to keep the tube vertical before pulling an egg out of his pocket and pressing the palm of his hand against the tube's opening, the egg resting inside. "And now!"

The entertainer turned the tube over and the egg fell. Instead of breaking at the bottom as Shirley had expected, however, the egg slowed to a stop midway down the tube. Nothing had caught it or slowed it down, at least not as far as Shirley could see. It had just stopped in midair of its own accord.

The audience oohed and aahed in appreciation while the entertainer showed off the mysterious floating egg, a big, toothy grin on his face.

"That's right, ladies and gentlemen. What you are witnessing right now is known as a vacuum. So long as the tube remains free of air, the egg will slow and stop before it can hit the bottom and break. And do you realize what these vacuums can do? Why, some of the greatest inventors and businessmen in this glorious empire are using vacuums to pump well water from deep beneath the Earth! The principles behind the vacuum and the pump are what allow the trains in the Underground and throughout the country to move from one place to another so fast. They suck and pull all the material in a space out until even the tiniest motes of dust are unable to stay in it! In the case of trains and wells, they are sucking and pulling water to create movement or to slake your thirst! That, ladies and gentlemen, boys and girls, is the wonder of the vacuum! The wonder of science!"

The audience, including Shirley, clapped enthusiastically. The entertainer beamed and bowed. "And over the next hour," he continued, "I will continue to demonstrate for you the wondrous scientific principles behind many things you take for granted! Perhaps someday, you'll take what you learn here and become the next great scientist or inventor! Now observe!"

While the entertainer set up his next science trick, Shirley slipped away and made her way inside. The science the man was demonstrating was interesting, but she had errands to run and what he was showing people did her no good, anyway. It was not as if his vacuums would help her clean faster or anything useful like that.

Shirley went about her shopping, moving between booths and shops as she sought out each item. To her relief, all that was required for Mrs. Avondale's dinner party tomorrow night was in stock, fresh, and even discounted in some places. By the time she left an hour later for the Underground, Shirley had plenty of change left. She was certain Mrs. Avondale, who could be quite tight-fisted at times, would be happy to receive so many coins back. She might even let Shirley keep a few. Doubtful, but one could hope!

As Shirley neared the station, a man pushing a cart piled high with books called out to her from the other side of the street. "Hello, pretty miss! Interested in some literature? We have the best romance novels, the latest stories from Robert Louis Stevenson and Jules Verne, and the pick of the lot for penny dreadfuls, both individual and collected!"

Despite knowing better—Shirley would be drawn into a conversation she was frankly uninterested in if she looked, and that might lead to being coerced into buying something off the cart with her own pocket money just to get rid of the bookseller—she turned her head in the cart's direction. Even from across the street, the books' titles jumped out at her in big, bold letters: *Claudius Bombernac*; *Poems by Alfred, Lord Tennyson*; *The Complete Works of Edgar Allen Poe*; *Carmilla*; *Wuthering Heights*; *Jane Eyre*; *A Christmas Carol*; *The Mudfrog Papers*; *No Thoroughfare*; and many more. However, it was the little bound booklets on tan or yellow paper with their lurid artwork underneath lurid titles, the penny dreadfuls, that drew her eye. How could they not? They were just so horrid.

A String of Pearls; or the Story of Sweeney Todd, the Demon Barber of Fleet Street: a demented-looking man with a twisted smile and a bloody straight razor in his hand grinned out at the world from the front cover. *Varney the Vampire; or the Feast of Blood*: a skeletal man wearing a sheet stood over a sleeping woman with a look somewhere between thirst and carnal lust on his face. And—

Mrs. Ripper, the Bloody Queen of Whitehall. The picture on the covered showed a beautiful, blushing bride linked arm-in-arm with a man whose face was half-human, half-demon. In his free hand, the man held a large butcher's knife dripping with blood. A subtitle underneath the picture proclaimed, *The True Story of Jack the Ripper, as Related by His Wife*.

Jack the Ripper.

Panic burst like a volcanic eruption in Shirley's chest and seized hold of her heart and lungs. Blood rushed loudly in her ears, and a cold sweat broke out over her. "Um...no, thank you, sir," she stammered to the bookseller. "I have to be off now. I'm needed at home."

She turned and ran towards the entrance to the Underground, ignoring the concerned cries of the bookseller and the stares of passersby. She nearly stumbled down the stairs, pushing her way through the crowds to get to the gate, pay her fee and rush through the gate. By the time she was on the train, her breathing was quick and shallow.

It took a few moments for her to realize that the other passengers were staring at her. A few were even whispering. She had to calm herself down, lest she bring shame upon herself and, by extension, the Avondale household for causing trouble in public. Closing her eyes, she tried to focus and steady on her breathing. From what she had heard as a girl, there were men in India who could breathe like this and achieve a state of grace on par with the divine bliss of the sainted. She had no idea if this was true, as she had never met an Indian man to ask, but it helped her calm down enough that she was able to breathe normally. More importantly, it stopped her from drawing stares.

This is all that bookseller's fault, Shirley thought, leaning back against her seat. *He called me pretty. I get called that so rarely*. Even as she thought that, though, she knew it was not true. It was not the bookseller's fault, but the fault of those horrid books. Especially that one volume she had noticed. *Mrs. Ripper; the Bloody Queen of Whitechapel*. That illustration. The Ripper.

Shirley rubbed her forehead as if to clear it. Even six years after those murders, they still had a hold over her. Especially after she had read those articles in *The Sun* last month. All her memories of those days came back to her so easily lately. Even cheap, silly books trying to profit off someone else's tragedy could send her into terror and remind her of when she lived in the Whitechapel area with her mum. Force her to remember things better left not thought of.

As the train rocked back and forth, she checked her bag to make sure none of the groceries had been disturbed, and that took her mind off the Ripper. Satisfied that all her purchases were still there and intact, she continued to quietly focus on her breathing until she reached her station. By the time she had emerged into the daylight again, Shirley had managed to push all those morbid thoughts away and was even able to hum a little as she made her way back to the Avondale house.

Then she spotted the police wagon in front of her place of employment. Her heart went cold.

Ignoring the normal rules which required her to enter through the back entrance, Shirley raced along the street, holding her skirt up in front of her as she went. By the time she reached the front stoop, her hair had come undone from under her hat, and she was panting. Nevertheless, when she noticed the front door was unlocked and slightly ajar, her strength returned tenfold and she burst through the front entrance, determined to find out what had happened.

Two surprised bobbies stared at her as she lost her balance and nearly fell to her knees. One of them asked who she was. She ignored them both as she saw Nellie and Lucinda sitting on the stairs, the latter sobbing and holding a handkerchief to her face. Lucinda's eyes fixed on Shirley and a fresh wave of tears gushed from her eyes.

"Oh Shirley!" she wailed, jumping up and running to her. Shirley had just enough time to straighten herself before Lucinda threw her arms around her and buried her head in the maid's bosom. Grabbing the wall for support, Shirley mechanically embraced the sobbing girl with her free arm. She had expected—well, she had not known what to expect. She had seen the police wagon sitting out front and had assumed the worst, she guessed. But Lucinda hugging and seeking support from her? Entirely unexpected. Shirley was unsure of how to react.

She turned to Nellie. "What happened?"

The younger maid, who looked to be on the verge of tears herself, sniffed and cleared her throat. "It happened just after you left," she explained. "The master picked up the missus. They left to see the missus's friend, turned onto another street and then..."

But whatever happened, Nellie couldn't continue and instead dissolved into tears, hiding her face in her sleeve. One of the bobbies finished for her. "There was a crash. It appears the axle on the cab was rotted through and chose that moment to break. The wheels fell out, the carriage went over and rolled down the street. Both...both occupants were pronounced dead at the scene."

Lucinda's wails gained new energy as the bobby finished and she squeezed Shirley tighter. Shirley rubbed her employer's daughter's back, unable to respond. Once again, death had come for someone she knew and, while it was nowhere near as horrible, it had been just as unexpected.

Chapter Two

Black crepe on the windows. Black crepe on the mirrors. Black crepe on any surface that could possibly hold a reflection. Black fabric over every surface in the drawing room, where the caskets were to be laid out. Black aprons over dark grey uniforms and new caps with black bands for the maids. An entire new wardrobe of black mourning garb for Lucinda, bought earlier this week from Black Peter Robinson's mourning warehouse. Black here. Black there. Black everywhere. A sea of black.

Since the carriage accident last week, Shirley and Nellie had put up the majority of the black to reflect the Avondale house's state of mourning. It was important, especially in families of good reputation and standing such as the Avondales, to display their mourning in everything from their dress, to the decoration of the household, to even their conduct. By the unwritten rules of mourning, Lucinda had to cut off all socializing so she could mourn and focus on her loss in peace. This period of mourning was to last, according to the standards of English society, about six months. Afterwards, Lucinda could slowly allow color back into her wardrobe and maybe socialize a little. Maybe.

Shirley did not know who had set these standards for mourning or why. When her mother had died, she had been too busy learning to be a maid to mourn, and she had not been close enough to her mother by then to feel anything, anyway. But Lucinda had been very close to her parents and they to her. Therefore, it was not just because of the custom that Lucinda was observing the mourning ritual. She needed to. Thus, Shirley and Nellie had hung up the black crepe and transformed the house into a dark and cheerless place. It was enough to make Shirley, who had not much cared for her employers, feel a pang of sadness at their passing.

Still, it was for the Avondale children, whom she had cared for even less, that Shirley felt most aggrieved. Lucinda, who had been a confident and snide young woman with a healthy appetite before the accident, had become quiet and withdrawn, and only picked at her food during meals. The poor girl had even taken to asking Shirley or Nellie to sleep in her bed with her at night, something Shirley only did because she felt sorry for the girl and did not want to cause her more upset. Thankfully, Nellie was more often willing than she was to sleep in Lucinda's room, so Shirley was spared having to do so most nights.

Griffin, however—

"Shirley, would you please come in here?"

Shirley, who had been dusting one of the vases on the second floor, jumped as she heard her name called. *Did he know I was thinking about him?* she wondered.

Steeling herself for what was to come, she strode over to the room that had formerly been Mr. Avondale's office. Now his son Griffin occupied it, along with Mr. Leopold, the Avondale family's solicitor, who had been visiting the home every day since Griffin had returned from Eton. What legal matters the passing of one's clients required so many daily visits, Shirley had no idea, but from the way both men holed themselves up there every day, it must be quite serious.

Both gentlemen stopped talking as she entered the office. The younger, Griffin Avondale, was dressed in a black dress shirt, black vest and had a black armband on his right sleeve. Mr. Leopold, on the other hand, wore a simple grey suit, the only evidence that he was mourning someone being the thin black armband on his coat sleeve.

"What may I do for you, Mister Griffin—I mean, Mr. Avondale?" Shirley corrected herself. Now that Griffin was the head of the household, she had to address him accordingly.

"Mr. Leopold is done for today," Griffin replied. "Would you please see him out?"

"Yes sir."

"And afterwards, would you please bring up a pot of tea?"

She stiffened. "Of course, sir."

Griffin and Mr. Leopold shook hands before the latter picked up his briefcase and followed Shirley out the door. After the solicitor was gone, she went to the kitchen, where Nellie was preparing a soup for supper that evening. The younger maid glanced up from the soup pot as Shirley walked in. There were red circles under her eyes.

"Nellie, have you been crying again?" Shirley asked.

She nodded and turned back to the broth. "I always get teary when someone I know dies," she explained. "My mum used to say it was one of God's gifts, that I could mourn for everyone who passed, no matter who they were or what they'd done in life."

Shirley had no idea how to respond to that, so instead she informed Nellie that Griffin had asked for a pot of tea. Nellie nodded and gestured her head at a large metal kettle sitting on the stove. "Just boiled some water for Miss Lucinda. Should I bring it up—?"

"No!" Shirley said quickly and a little louder than necessary. She coughed. "I mean, I'll take care of it. You handle the broth, alright?"

Nellie did not comment on Shirley's odd demeanor, but instead turned back to her soup. Taking a deep breath, Shirley gathered a teapot, cup, and saucer, threw some tea leaves into a strainer, and poured hot water through the strainer and into the pot. She then carried all three items on a sliver tray upstairs, stealing herself again for another meeting alone with Griffin Avondale.

As she entered the office, taking care to keep the door open, Griffin looked up from a letter he was writing. "Just set it on the desk, Shirley," he said.

"Yes sir." She placed the tray down, turned to go, and felt a large hand engulf her tiny wrist, followed by a pair of lips on the back of her hand. Her head whipped round, and her eyes fell on Griffin, who was staring at her with a gaze she had never seen directed at her from anyone else.

"Mr. Avondale—!"

"Shirley, have you thought at all about my offer?" he asked.

She snatched her hand back. Griffin, in response, stood, shortened the gap between them and grabbed her by the shoulders. His face was a portrait of earnestness.

"Mr. Avondale!" Shirley repeated.

"Please Shirley," he replied. "I love you. Marry me."

She stared up at his face. He was handsome, with blonde hair that was long enough to be rebellious but not too long to be improper, an angular face, and expressive blue eyes. It was enough to make any girl swoon in his arms.

Which was why she hadn't allowed Nellie to bring the tea up for him. Shirley hated to think what might happen if Griffin made advances on the younger maid like this.

She twisted free from his grip and glared at him furiously. "Mr. Avondale, you shouldn't make jokes like that!"

"I wasn't joking."

"All the more reason not to say it," she replied.

"When will you take me seriously?" he asked.

Shirley crossed her arms in front of her chest. She would not back down.

Perhaps in the world of novels, relationships between servants and their masters could occur. Perhaps in those worlds, or even in far off places like America, India or the Australian continent, romantic love might actually exist. They may even, on occasion and despite all opposition, prosper.

But Shirley lived in the real world, in London, and she knew that romantic love was just a fairy tale for upper class women and girls to sigh over. The reality was every marriage was a match made by considerations other than love, and it was without love that she considered marriage, on the rare occasion when it came up, to anyone. It was with those other considerations she had considered Griffin Avondale's proposal the first time he'd made it, after she'd begun working for his family and he'd been home from school for holiday.

Obviously, she had said no.

The first problem with Griffin's suit was that Shirley was a maid and Griffin was the son of a drill manufacturer. Well, technically he was now the drill manufacturer, though he had no say in the running of his company yet. But that only widened the gap between them. Griffin would be expected to marry the daughter of another wealthy businessman, or perhaps one of the daughters of a nobleman, if the match was advantageous to the nobleman's family as well.

What was Shirley compared to one of those glittering ladies? Just a maid, the daughter of a no-account unmarried drunk from the infamous Whitechapel neighborhood. She was much too far below his social station. Their union would ruin him socially, which would likely inhibit his business and financial prospects and send them into poverty.

And then there was Griffin himself. She did not know him very well, because he was usually at Eton College instead of at home with his family. But he was now her master as well as the son of her former master, and she knew the risks. Any maid who went to work in a house where a man lived had heard the stories. Men would seduce their maids, promising them everything they ever wanted, all to get them into their bedsheets. Sometimes they did not even bother with the seducing. Sometimes they just took them to the bedsheets, whether the maid wanted them or not.

The result, inevitably, was the same. The maid would end up pregnant and forced out of her job. The man of the house would abandon her and go on about his merry life, perhaps only inconvenienced by his wife's accusing eyes and cold silence. Meanwhile, the maid would be declared a fallen woman, which was only a thinly veiled accusation of being a prostitute. She would be shunned from any job as well as from respectable society and would have no means to care for herself or her baby once it was born. The story usually ended with a back-alley abortion, the baby being sold off to someone, alcoholism, the maid resorting to prostitution so she could earn money for food, the baby dying, the maid dying, or some combination of all the above.

In short, Griffin Avondale was a man whom Shirley could not afford to become entangled with. If he were serious with his feelings towards her, they would likely lose more than they gained by their union. And if he were not, she would be abandoned once his lust was sated and forced to fend for herself with his bastard while he courted ladies more in line with his status.

And if she had to guess, Griffin was not serious about his intentions. *After all*, a dark voice in the back of Shirley's head reminded her, *what would he want with a low-class girl with a funny eye?*

Griffin was waiting for her answer. Shirley took another deep breath and calculated how best to phrase her rejection without losing her job. "Forgive me Mr. Avondale, but I'm afraid you and I are ill-matched for one another. I suggest we both look for more appropriate prospects in other quarters." And with that, she turned and walked as fast as she could out of the office.

"Wait Shirley!" Griffin called. Footsteps clattered behind her, and she was sure he was going to grab her again and pull her back into the office. She turned around to fend him off—

From below, there were three sharp raps on the door. Shirley stopped mid-turn, and Griffin stopped mid-stride. She coughed. "Excuse me, Mr. Avondale." She headed down the stairs and to the door. From her bedroom on the second floor, she heard Lucinda's door open behind her.

"Who's visiting now?" she called.

Shirley reached the door and opened it. "Avondale residence," she recited, examining the new arrival.

On the stoop was a man she had never seen before. He was tall and thin, with a sunken face and long, brown hair slicked back from his forehead with some sort of pomade. He wore a smart suit that, along with the carriage sitting on the street behind him and the way he held himself up, hinted that this man was of high class. Maybe even nobility.

And the grave expression on his face warned that he did not care for silliness or to be kept waiting.

"May I help you?" Shirley asked nervously.

"I'm here to see the Avondale children," said the gentleman.

"I can take your card, sir—" Shirley began. Normally, instead of actually meeting with the mourners, well-wishers left cards to indicate that they had stopped by and were thinking of the family. It was a good way to show you cared without having to make yourself uncomfortable with the ever-present specter of death.

"I am not here to leave a card like the other well-wishers," the man interrupted. "I am Sir Joseph Gregory Hunting, the third baronet of the House of Hunting, as well as family to the deceased. And I will see my great-nephew and niece."

Shirley raised an eyebrow. Sir Joseph Gregory Hunting? Baronet of the House of Hunting? Great-nephew and niece? Lucinda had told her during one of the nights they had spent together that she and her brother had no other family. Also, were not baronets a type of nobility? Yes, she was sure of that. They were lower than barons, but they still had titles and land and all the other fancy things that came with being born noble. If that was the case, surely Mrs. Avondale, who was always seeking to move her family up higher in society, would have mentioned a connection to a noble house, let alone informed her daughter of that fact. Could this man be some sort of imposter? A confidence man who wanted to take advantage of two young and desperate mourners?

"Let him in, Shirley," said a voice behind her. She turned to see Griffin and Lucinda descending the stairs. The older Avondale glared suspiciously at the new arrival, while the younger, dressed entirely in black, kept glancing between her brother and this man claiming to be her relative with confusion.

Orders given, Shirley stepped aside. The man entered and appraised the siblings with his eyes.

"I do not believe we have been introduced," said the man as Shirley shut the door behind him. "I am Sir Joseph Gregory Hunting—"

"I know who you are," Griffin cut in.

"I do not know him," Lucinda said in a small voice. "Who is he?"

"I am the Baronet of House Hunting," Sir Joseph answered. "As well as your mother's uncle."

"Mother never said she had an uncle," Lucinda murmured.

"She told me," Griffin revealed. When Lucinda turned to him with eyes full of uncertainty and hurt, he explained, "Mother believed it was better for you not to know. Apparently, her uncle is something of a scoundrel who has driven off everyone close to him. Not to mention he spends all his time experimenting with odd sciences. Some of which could be deemed occult."

He said all this with distrustful eyes pointed at Sir Joseph. For his part, Sir Joseph remained unperturbed by the accusations. "I do admit, people who concern themselves with gossip and superficial matters have reason to be concerned over me," the baronet replied. "My wife died, as well as my son and daughter. All three died untimely deaths. And instead of trying to find a replacement for my wife to produce replacement heirs, as some of the other gentlemen of British society would have done, I decided to devote myself to more fruitful pursuits." He made a face that left no question of how he felt regarding the route the other gentlemen of British society would have taken. "Misunderstandings regarding my decisions have, as you can see, led to obnoxious and baseless rumors about me and my activities. Not to mention, the slander to my reputation has led to my estrangement from my closest family members."

"And you're here to fix that estrangement?" Griffin asked, his suspicions clearly not assuaged.

"I am here because my niece and her husband died. Even if I was not welcome in their company during their lifetimes, I will at the very least pay my respects afterwards." He fixed Griffin with a contemptuous glare. "Especially when one of my niece's children is in need of care, and the other can't provide that care."

Griffin stared at Sir Joseph, aghast. "What do you mean by that?"

"Do not think I'm unaware, young man," Sir Joseph replied. "Your father owned the company he helped to found, but you have no ownership over it, do you? If my sources are correct, the board of directors has elected to cut the Avondale family off entirely once they have finished handing over control of the company to its new president. Am I wrong?"

All eyes turned to Griffin, who had the face of a man recently shot in the chest. Lucinda's eyes were welling with tears. "Griffin, is that true?"

"No, it's not!" Griffin spat. "Mr. Leopold and I are working on regaining control of the company. And once we're done—!"

"Once you are done, the company will still be in the hands of its current president and both you and your sister will have lost everything paying fees for Mr. Leopold." Sir Joseph's face remained impassive, while Griffin had that shot expression again. "And what if you are required by the courts to pay the company's solicitor's fees? Please, young man. I may be considered eccentric by the standards of our society, but I am not a fool. Even I realize this will be a difficult case at best. Mr. Leopold probably made you aware of all that, did he not?"

"He...well, he...I—"

Griffin appeared on the verge of joining his sister in weeping. Shirley could tell he was struggling to keep himself under control despite the roil of emotions he was feeling.

Sir Joseph nodded as if confirming something he'd always known. "Your father probably hoped that you would marry well enough to live a life of leisure. It is a familiar story. Many fathers in the upper strata of

England work hard and build business empires with the hope that their sons will never have to work when they reach adulthood, let alone run those empires. They were doing that in my grandfather's generation. It is only unfortunate that your father did not live long enough to see his plans grow to fruition."

"You leave my father out of this!" Griffin almost roared.

"Does that mean we will have to sell our home?" Lucinda asked. "Everything we own?"

Shirley had been wondering the same thing as well. She was no expert, but she knew her numbers and had done her own finances for years. A house the size of the Avondale's required at least two competent maids to keep clean. Then there were any repairs that needed to be done to the home or anything inside. The gas company had to be paid once a month. And of course, there were necessities such as food and toiletries. All those costs could pile up after a while.

Which begged the question: how long could Griffin afford to keep her employed before she would have to find work elsewhere? Hopefully, long enough for him to write a letter of recommendation. Without one of those from a previous employer, it was extremely difficult for maids to find new situations. Some even became destitute without steady means of work and had to look for other means to support themselves. Marriage, perhaps, or working in a pub or coffeehouse. Some turned to prostitution or begging.

And a few, those with no other choices and despairing of any hope, went to the workhouses.

Shirley thought she would kill herself before she turned to one of those places for help. On the surface, they were supposed to offer charity, warm beds and food, and training for jobs. But in the reality, they were often cold, underfunded, run by the cruelest of men and women, and left any who entered with a more damaging mark than the one God placed upon Cain. Indeed, some who entered workhouses to find work ended up never finding work, or their dignity, ever again.

But there was time enough to consider new positions and workhouses later. Shirley turned her attention back to Griffin, who was struggling with how to answer his sister's tear-filled question. He was saved from this predicament by Sir Joseph clearing his throat. "Lucky for you, I may have a solution to your situation."

"You do?" said Lucinda hopefully.

"What is it?" Griffin asked warily.

"Young Lucinda should be with family," Sir Joseph explained. "I am family. She can come live with me at Hunting Lodge—that is the name of our family estate. My grandfather had a sense of humor, as you can imagine. Anyway, she can live with me, and you can use your remaining funds to go to Oxford or wherever it was you were accepted for university."

"No," said Griffin.

"But Griffin—!" Lucinda began.

"I said no!"

"Do you really have any other choice?" asked Sir Joseph, his voice indicating that there was no other choice and they all knew it.

Griffin opened his mouth to say something, but Lucinda placed a hand on his arm and gave him a meaningful look. The young man closed his mouth, groaned, and finally murmured, "Give us time to discuss it."

They disappeared up the stairs and into the office, leaving Shirley alone with Sir Joseph. Remembering that she was still the Avondales' maid, she turned to the elderly baronet and said, "May I show you to the drawing room while you wait, sir?"

"Please," Sir Joseph replied.

Shirley led Sir Joseph into the drawing room. The baronet glanced around at the black crepe and then sat down on the French couch. Whether or not he approved of how his late niece and her husband had decorated their home, Shirley could not say.

"Would you like a cup of tea, sir?" she asked.

He nodded, and she left for the kitchen. When she got there, she found Nellie waiting for her, eyes alight with excitement and consternation.

"What's with all the shouting out there?" she asked. "Who's the man in the fancy clothes you showed into the drawing room? I couldn't hear anything from here!"

"But you were watching?" Shirley asked, eyebrow raised.

Nellie immediately realized her mistake and blushed. "Just a peek to see what all the fuss was about."

Shirley sighed. "Put a kettle on, and I'll tell you. Come on, quick-like!"

By the time the tea was ready, Nellie was caught up and was gazing at Shirley with eyes full of concern. "So, what's going to happen to us? I mean, if the Master can't afford to pay us no more?"

Shirley didn't answer. Instead, she took the tray with the teapot and cup on it and carried it out to the kitchen, leaving Nellie to stew in her own worry. Sir Joseph was in the same spot she had left him, looking horribly bored with his wait.

"Your tea, sir," she announced, laying the tray down before him.

"Thank you, Shirley," he replied. "It is Shirley, isn't it?"

"Um, yes sir. Shirley Dobbins, sir." She straightened, not used to being addressed by guests in such a manner, let alone guests of such high station. Normally guests would let Mr. or Mrs. Avondale know what they needed, and they would tell Nellie to have Shirley prepare it in the kitchen, where her lazy eye was not a problem.

Speaking of which, was Sir Joseph staring at her eye? Was he upset by it?

"Your eye," he said then. "Was it like that at birth?"

"I-I think so, sir," she answered, inwardly flinching. She wished she could sink into the floor, as she had every day since childhood, when other children would make fun of her eye.

"Does it cause issues in your work?"

"Not that I'm aware of, sir," she replied. "I mean, no one has found any fault in my work before because of my eye."

"Really?" he said, keen interest splayed across his face. She blushed, feeling like an exhibit in one of those traveling freak shows she had heard of. "How long have you been working as a maid?"

"Six years this November, sir."

"Six years! So, you were how old when you started?"

"Ten, sir."

A sudden thought occurred to her: could Sir Joseph be interested in her in the same way Griffin was? Did he perhaps prefer girls around her age with deformities like hers? Maybe it was a familial trait passed along the males of Mrs. Avondale's family. It would go a long way to explain some things.

Before she could reason it out any further, however, there was a clatter of feet on the stairs. Griffin and Lucinda reappeared. The former still looked ready for a confrontation, while the latter seemed hopeful for the first time since her parents had died.

"Alright, Sir Joseph," said Griffin. "We have decided to accept your proposal, on one condition."

"Oh, don't look so serious, boy. I'm not going to hurt your precious sister. What do you want?"

"First, I shall be living with you as well," he replied. "Not always, just during the holidays. And as soon as I'm able to support my sister, you will allow her to leave and live with me if she so wishes."

"Fine," he said, speaking with the air of a man who had been expecting something like this. "I had planned to open my home to you in any case. Anything else?"

"No, that will be all."

"Th-Thank you, Uncle," Lucinda uttered nervously. "We appreciate your generosity."

Sir Joseph, however, acted as if he hadn't heard her. He turned to Shirley. "How would you like to come work for me at Hunting Lodge?"

Shirley felt her eyes go as wide as dinner plates. Across the room, she noticed similar surprise on Griffin and Lucinda's faces. "M-Me, sir?"

"My staff tells me they need another maid if they are to keep Hunting Lodge livable," he replied, speaking as if this were an annoying triviality he was only mentioning just to get it out of the way. "And from the appearance of this house, you seem to have all the skills my housekeeper could ask for, despite your condition. Or is this house's upkeep due to another in the house?"

Shirley thought of Nellie and shook her head. "No sir. I lead the housekeeping in this house."

"Shirley has been acting as our head housekeeper since Sarah Fagan retired some months ago," Griffin explained.

"Excellent!" Sir Joseph clapped his hands together. "I can pay you seven pounds a year. How does that sound?"

Shirley felt her heart skip a beat. "Seven pounds?"

"Fine, eight. I will not go any higher, though."

Eight pounds a year? Shirley had to put a hand on a table to keep herself from fainting. That was well above what Mrs. Avondale paid her as a maid-of-all-work. And on a baronet's estate, no less! The upwards progression for her if she worked hard and was successful at a place such as Sir Joseph's knew no limits!

But what about your new employer?

The voice in Shirley's head raised a good point. He had seemed overly interested in her eye, and there was still the possibility that he held the same sort of fascination with her as Griffin did. If, once she was at his estate, his odd attentions continued, what would she do?

"Please say you will come, Shirley!" Lucinda threw herself at Shirley, eyes wide and pleading as she desperately grabbed at her sleeves. "I want you to come! Please say you will join us at the Hunting Lodge!"

This time, Shirley had to grab both the table and the mantlepiece above the fireplace to stay steady. *What is with this girl lately?* she wondered.

Griffin said something as well about her working for his great-uncle, but she did not catch it. All she heard was the baronet's words: "I will need a decision before I leave, please."

And like that, she decided. To the baronet, she said, "Yes sir. I would be more than grateful to come work at your estate."

Griffin smiled, while Lucinda gave a very unladylike cheer and buried her face in Shirley's bosom again. Sir Joseph's mouth twitched upwards in a smile. "Excellent. Now Griffin, shall we sit down and discuss the details of you and your sister's move to Hunting Lodge?"

The men sat down to discuss while Shirley led Lucinda out of the drawing room, the latter gabbing away at her about how excited she was for Shirley to join them. She paid no attention to the noise, however; she was too busy trying to figure out what to tell Nellie. From their conversation, she had a feeling Sir Joseph would not want to take on such an inexperienced maid to his estate. It would fall to Shirley to break the bad news to the younger girl, and she was not looking forward to it.

Chapter Three

The carriage rocked and rattled as it flew down the dirt road towards Sir Joseph Hunting's estate. Staring out the window, Shirley could not have thought of a more dismal day for them to set out for the Hunting Lodge. The sky was overcast and threatening to drop a torrent of rain at any second. This was her first time leaving the confines of London, and she could not help but feel this was some sort of sign of things to come.

The question is, she thought, *who is the omen for? For me, or for them?*

She glanced at the two other occupants of the carriage, the Avondale siblings. Griffin was seated diagonally from her, gazing out the opposite window at nothing. Lucinda sat beside him and across from Shirley, still dabbing her eyes with a lace handkerchief.

Only a few hours before, she and Griffin had taken one last look at their home, the only home they had ever known and had said goodbye before leaving for the country with Shirley. Lucinda had cried plenty already after watching many of her family's possessions, the ones that weren't coming with them, sold or auctioned off these past several days. But the tears she had shed as the carriage had ridden away had been so passionate and unending, not to mention so loud, that Shirley had wondered where the water to make the tears were coming from! It certainly could not come from Lucinda alone.

Still, while she could only imagine what Lucinda and Griffin were going through, she could sympathize. Shirley had had to move several times by the time she started working as a maid, and all her worldly possessions fit into one battered yellow suitcase. For her, home was wherever she could lay her head down, and had nothing to do with happy memories or length of time spent there.

The death of her mother had only affected her slightly more than the multiple moves. Yes, Shirley had shed a couple of tears when Mary Dobbins had passed, but plenty of women died of drink and disease every day, and there had been work to do. Shirley had not the time nor energy to grieve for her mother, though she had felt sorry for her and other women who had lived and died that way.

Contrast that to Griffin and Lucinda Avondale, who had been close to their parents and had lost them in a tragic accident, followed by losing their precious home not long after. It must have felt like their worlds had fallen apart.

Well, at least they have family who is willing to take them in, Shirley thought. And this family member was willing to give her employment on top of that. And a baronet, no less! Already, she was imagining what new heights her career could lead to while working in the home of a baronet. If she did well there, she could ascend the ranks to head maid, and then to head housekeeper. Or she could achieve those positions in a new household, one higher in rank than the baronet's. Maybe even an earl or a marquis's home!

"What do you think our new home will be like?"

Shirley pulled herself out of her fantasies. She'd almost forgotten that she was in a carriage with a pair of mourners. How horrible would they think she was if they caught her daydreaming with a smile on her face while they sat in misery? For once, Shirley was grateful for Lucinda's presence.

Griffin sighed and turned away from the window. "I understand it to be a fairly large manor, built in what people call the Georgian style, so there will likely be lots of symmetry and columns in the design of the house. As the style suggests, it was built in the era of King George—the Third, I think—and was designed by Edward Blore, who would later go on to design Buckingham Palace, among other famous landmarks."

Lucinda laughed; it was the first Shirley had heard from her since her parents' passing. "You sound like a tourist guide. Anything else you can tell us?"

"I believe Sir Joseph—I mean, I believe Uncle Joseph said the land around the Lodge comprises of several farms and a few small villages.

They pay him rent and a portion of the harvest every year, which is where he gets most of his income. Other than that, I do not know much else. Except that that the border into his land is marked by two stone pillars. One of the pillars is headed by the statue of a hawk in flight, the other a hunting dog in mid-leap."

"Hunting animals," said Shirley, speaking for the first time.

Griffin nodded. "They mark the Hunting family crest as well. I think Mother said a relief of that crest is shown somewhere on the outside of the house. Over the door, most likely."

The atmosphere in the carriage took on a morose aspect at Mrs. Avondale's mention, and the siblings fell into silence. Shirley, not exactly sad for the silence, continued to gaze out the window. Neither she nor the siblings commented when the pillars, topped with a flying hawk and a leaping foxhound as Griffin had said, passed by.

Another quiet hour passed. When their destination came into view, however, Lucinda leaned against the window and nearly shouted, "There it is! There it is!"

Indeed, there it was, a red brick edifice with three floors in its box-like central wing and a pair of L-shaped wings with two floors each extending from its north and south sides. To Shirley, it looked like the central house had grown arms, especially with the shape of the wings and their sharply slanted roofs covered in coal-gray slate. Marble columns adorned the building where walls met, and a giant family crest, also made of marble, hung above an ornate stoop.

"It's lovely," Lucinda murmured.

"It will do," Griffin commented dismissively.

It's big, thought Shirley. *Bigger than any house I've ever worked in. Still, the outside looks plenty clean, so it seems well cared for. No ivy, either. And—*

While examining the house with her maid's eye, she noticed something off about the place. Four chimneys popped out of each corner of the central building, while two more rose out of each wing.

While the chimneys in the central building and on the south wing were sending smoke up to the heavens, only one chimney smack dab in the middle of the north wing appeared to be lit. She found that curious. Usually if one fireplace were lit, all of them would be, especially on a cold and dreary day like today. Was there a special reason the one at the end of the north wing had been left unlit?

The carriage pulled to a stop in front of the Lodge, where two figures, a man and a woman, stood on the stoop waiting for them. Shirley noted that Sir Joseph was not among them. This also struck her as odd, especially considering the baronet's avowal of family duty. After all, if they could see the house from a distance, anyone in the house would have seen them and gone to notify their master. He had had ample time to make it to the front stoop.

So why had he not come?

The driver of the carriage came around and opened the door. Griffin stepped out first, then helped Lucinda and Shirley disembark. As they looked around, the man on the stoop approached and bowed low. From his age and his uniform, Shirley clocked him immediately as Sir Joseph's butler.

"Welcome to the Hunting Lodge," he said, his voice tinged with an accent that identified him as originally from Kent. "My name is James Milverton. I am the butler to Sir Joseph. This is Mrs. Angela Preston, our head housekeeper."

"Welcome, Mr. Avondale," she said in a perfect Queen's English. She bowed to Griffin and then to Lucinda. "Miss Avondale."

The siblings nodded at them. Mrs. Preston then turned to Shirley. "You must be Shirley Dobbins. You'll be coming with me once we get inside."

"Thank you, ma'am," Shirley replied, appraising the woman. Immediately, she decided this was someone to look up to. Mrs. Preston had a quiet strength and dignity in her bearing, one that Shirley sensed came from having worked years in her profession and gotten good at it. Exactly the kind of person Shirley wanted to be in ten years, in the position she wanted to hold in fifteen or twenty. "I look forward to working with you."

"Where's Uncle Joseph?" asked Lucinda, her eyes wide and searching, like a timid rabbit on the lookout for danger.

Milverton and Mrs. Preston glanced at one another. Then the elderly butler coughed into his gloved fist. "Sir Joseph will be along shortly. He had some work to take care of in the laboratory."

"The laboratory?" Griffin repeated, eyebrow raised.

"How about we get you and your things inside?" Milverton snapped his fingers, and three men in work clothes appeared from out of nowhere. They grabbed the luggage off the top of the carriage and carried it inside. One of the workmen noticed Shirley had her suitcase in her hands and offered to take it in. She politely declined, and the man shrugged before grabbing another suitcase from atop the carriage. When all the luggage had been brought in, Milverton and Mrs. Preston led Griffin, Lucinda and Shirley inside after the workmen.

"My Lord," said Griffin.

"My Lord" was right: while the outside had been well-presented and clean, the inside was dark and dirty. The walls were covered in moldy wallpaper, strips of which had peeled away from the walls; the floorboards were scuffed and needed a new coat of lacquer; and in the back of the foyer, where two adjacent staircases led to the second floors of the north and south wings, several rails were missing. Those that were still there looked like they'd seen better days. Spiderwebs filled several dark and out-of-reach corners, and the mirror above a soot-stained fireplace was spotted and cracked so that you could not see your reflection at all.

From a professional standpoint, Shirley was appalled. One could hardly tell that a staff worked here, judging by the upkeep. The only things she could find that appeared to be well-taken care of were the electric lights, which were glowing brightly from several wall sconces and from the chandelier above their heads.

"Why is this place so...so...?" Lucinda was unable to finish the question.

Milverton cleared his throat again. "Come now, I shall show you to your rooms, and then we will give you the grand tour of the house."

As the butler led Griffin and Lucinda towards one of the back stairways, Shirley followed Mrs. Preston down a hallway leading to the building's south wing. When they were out of earshot, Mrs. Preston whispered, "I bet you're wondering at the state of the manor."

"Um..."

"Oh, no denying it, dear," said Mrs. Preston, now speaking with a strong West Midlands accent. She gestured at the hallway they were walking through, which was in a similar state to that of the foyer. "I can see you looking about. Noticed the state of the house and everything?"

"Y-Yes ma'am," she replied, taken aback by the change of accent. She cleared her throat. "I mean, yes ma'am, I noticed the state of the house."

"Horrid state of things, isn't it? Looks like a place that writer Poe might set a story, it does." Mrs. Preston sighed. "But it didn't always used to look like this, you know. I began working at the Lodge in Sir Joseph's father's day. When Sir Gregory was alive, we had about forty members of staff, twenty of them maids, whose duties were to keep this house in top condition. Now we only have ten folks on staff full-time, and four of them work in the grounds or stables."

Shirley's mouth dropped. "Only six people work in the house?" Her mind reeled at the prospect. A house of this size, with high ceilings and hard to reach corners no less, would be impossible for four maids and a butler to maintain on their own. At least not in a state suitable for a baronet's home.

"Seven, now that you're here," said Mrs. Preston. "James and I head the staff. Hilly and Beth are the other two maids. And then there's Garland the cook and Luke, his son. The men you saw today were brought up from the Closer Village to help bring in the luggage. We weren't sure how much Mr. and Miss Avondale were bringing, so we thought a couple of extra hands would be good. But the three of you didn't bring much, did you? Sorry to say, James wasted his own pocket money."

"But in a house of this size...why doesn't Sir Joseph hire more staff?"

"Oh, he doesn't believe we need more staff," Mrs. Preston replied with a dismissive wave of her hand. "Says as long as the house is standing and no one's getting killed from falling ceiling beams, we don't need to hire anyone. Or do any major repair work, for that matter. Which is why, as you can see, this house is in such a state. Mind you, Sir Gregory would never have stood for this. He loved this house and enjoyed showing it off to guests. But Sir Joseph...well, you're here, my dear, and that's all that matters. We would've preferred he'd brought more than just one maid on board, but I suppose we shouldn't look a gift horse in the mouth. Ah, here we are."

They went down a staircase to a basement hallway. From the numerous doors on both sides of the hall, Shirley guessed this was the servants' quarters. A moment later she was proven right as Mrs. Preston pulled out a set of keys and unlocked the second nearest door on the left, revealing a small bedroom with two thin, narrow beds, a washstand, and a small wardrobe.

"This shall be yours, dear," she said. "Take whichever bed you like. Used to have to bunk two or three to a room in the old days. Sir Gregory was even talking about building a separate house for the servants, but...well, no sense on dwelling on the could-have-beens and maybes, now is there? You remember your way back to the foyer? Good. Meet me there in ten minutes. I've put your new uniform in the bottom drawer there."

As Mrs. Preston headed off, Shirley glanced around the room. It seemed in a better state than the rest of the house, with no cobwebs, grime or peeling wallpaper. It did have the air of a room that had not seen much use recently, but Shirley was fine with that. At least she could retreat here. Retreat here to her room after trying to make this place presentable—

Then she realized something: this was the first room Shirley had ever had that was all her own. No fellow maids or cockroaches. Just her. And with furnishings, to boot! A bed, a wardrobe and a washstand!

Shirley stood there, letting this new fact wash over her. *My own room*, she thought. *Well, even if this job ends up being terrible, at least I'll have a place of my own to sleep.*

She let herself enjoy this unexpected gift for a minute before emptying her suitcase and placing her clothes and possessions in the wardrobe. The process took less than two minutes. With that done, she changed into her new uniform, a black dress with a white apron and frilly white cap and headed back to the foyer. As she arrived, she spotted Lucinda stomping out of the north wing, across the foyer, and up the stairs to the north wing's second floor, her expression stormy. Griffin followed her a moment later, looking tired beyond all measure. He barely glanced at Shirley or Mrs. Preston, who was standing at the foot of the staircase, as he went after his sister.

"What do you suppose all that was about?" Mrs. Preston asked as soon as Griffin was out of earshot and Shirley had joined her by the stairs.

I have an idea, Shirley thought. *Lucinda's back to her old self again. And something didn't go her way just now.*

She had seen this scene play out before more than once at the Avondale residence in London: Lucinda would want something or want to go somewhere or see some friend or another. Usually, Mr. and Mrs. Avondale did not mind giving their daughter anything she wanted. In fact, they seemed to regard doing so as a sign that they were exemplary parents.

But on the rare occasion they did say "no," the subsequent tantrum would be legendary. It did not matter the reason her parents said no, even if the reason was legitimate. Nor did it matter how trivial Lucinda's request was. The moment she was denied, she would slam her feet, shout and cry, and when her parents held firm, as they always did when this happened, she would stomp off to her room and refuse to come out. It could be days until she reemerged, and even then, the silence she would gift her parents with could stretch out for weeks.

Shirley did not mind the tantrums—she was rarely around for them and enjoyed being left alone afterwards by the sullen Lucinda. But it obviously had bothered her parents. More than once, her employers had discussed sending Lucinda to a hospital for these tantrums. Mr. Avondale was of the opinion that this sort of behavior in a young woman, particularly for such trivial reasons and against all logical reasons provided to her, was not normal. He had even mentioned, in a voice barely above a whisper, that Lucinda's tantrums "could potentially be a sign of some sort of mental hysteria."

A sign of hysteria or not, Mrs. Avondale had always put her foot down and refused to send her daughter anywhere for any sort of treatment. In the end, her worry for her family's social standing and Lucinda's marriage prospects should it be realized she'd been sent to a hospital always outweighed her worry for her daughter's health. Mrs. Avondale would then close the subject with the assurance that Lucinda would outgrow her wilder moods before any suitors came by, and the discussion would be tabled until the next tantrum occurred.

Shirley had been at more than one of these conversations, normally serving the Avondales tea or sherry while they talked. Neither Mr. nor Mrs. Avondale had thought to send her away while they had these discussions. After all, good servants kept their masters' secrets, no matter what. And both of them agreed, Shirley was a good servant.

Not that she was going to tell Mrs. Preston all this. Even though she was now working for Sir Joseph at the Hunting Lodge, gossiping about her previous masters was still taboo. Indeed, doing so would more than likely give Mrs. Preston a bad impression of her. Rather, she would keep quiet and wait for the housekeeper to figure out Lucinda's quirks herself. If she was asked later and it was appropriate to do so, Shirley might explain Lucinda's behavior to the head housekeeper. She would be careful to choose her words, of course. Blunt speaking rarely mixed well with a servants' profession.

At that moment, Milverton appeared from the north wing, looking even more exhausted than Griffin had. "It would appear we have our work cut out for us," he said as he spotted Shirley and Mrs. Preston and crossed the foyer.

"What happened?" asked the housekeeper.

"Sir Joseph and Miss Lucinda had something of a disagreement," he replied. "And while I would never eavesdrop on matters between our master and his family, I was given to understand that the argument stemmed from the state of the house."

In other words, he was there for the entire argument and is itching to tell someone about it, Shirley thought. Sure enough, after a bit of prompting from Mrs. Preston, Milverton coughed and related what he had overheard.

"Well, Sir Joseph saw the young master and mistress in the parlor, and after thanking him for taking them in, Lucinda asked why the Lodge is in its current state. The master then became angry and replied that he had more important matters requiring his attention than whether a crack in the ceiling had been filled in. His words, not mine.

"Miss Lucinda then asked how she was supposed to socialize or have guests at this manor when the building was in such a state, and Sir Joseph replied it was no matter of his and she was free to do whatever she wanted, but to leave him out of it. You know how he is, Mrs. Preston: he dislikes crowds and socializing. He also let her know that as long as he was master of the Hunting Lodge, there would be no balls in his house, and that the ballroom itself was off-limits to them both."

"Why is the ballroom off-limits?" asked Shirley, unable to restrain herself. She knew for a fact that Lucinda dreamed of the day when she could enter a high society ball and dance with the eligible young bachelors there. To be denied the chance to have one of her own, particularly since a manor of this size which would likely have a spacious ballroom, would no doubt have been a slap in the face to her.

"Because dear, that's where Sir Joseph set up his laboratory," Mrs. Preston answered, rolling her eyes. "He runs experiments with all sorts of strange chemicals and machines and reads the strangest books in that room. Which he always keeps dark with the curtains drawn, by the way. Fears prying eyes. We're only allowed in there to drop off food, and even then, he wants us out as fast as possible. These days, he's building some sort of giant machine in there, though God only knows what the blasted thing is supposed to do."

"And when Miss Lucinda was told what he uses the ballroom for, she became quite upset," Milverton added, which Shirley understood to mean she had one of her famous tantrums. "She demanded that Sir Joseph think about his family's position in society and consider moving his scientific pursuits elsewhere. Of course, the master became quite heated and refused. He then warned his niece and nephew that while they may be his family, he only took them in for his own personal reasons, and he could kick them just as easily."

"And Miss Lucinda ran off after that?" Shirley guessed.

Milverton nodded. "Master Griffin followed shortly thereafter. I believe he tried to defuse the situation between his sister and the master during their argument, but his attempts were unsuccessful. And once Sir Joseph threatened to expel them from the house...well, you understand the situation. Anyway, Sir Joseph is back in the laboratory now. I better go see him before speaking with Mr. Garland about supper tonight."

Milverton turned and headed back the way he came. Mrs. Preston sighed and turned to Shirley. "Come along dear, we still have a tour of the house to give you."

Shirley followed Mrs. Preston out of the foyer, a sinking feeling in her heart. Somehow, she did not think this would be as wondrous a job as she had hoped for.

***

That evening, after learning the layout of the house, meeting the other staff members, and learning about the villages on the property (which had the very unimaginative names of the Closer Village and the Farther Village, based on their proximity to the Lodge), Shirley had served at an extremely uncomfortable dinner for Sir Joseph and the Avondale siblings. It was the most awkward meal Shirley had ever had the pleasure of serving. The diners spoke very little and looked at each other even less. And after clearing his plate, Sir Joseph left without a word, presumably to the ballroom and his experiments. Lucinda had left in a huff not too long afterwards, and then Griffin had apologized to Shirley and Mrs. Preston before leaving as well.

After the table had been cleared and the dishes cleaned, Shirley trudged her way to her room, somehow more exhausted than she had ever been at the Avondale household. And despite how the day had not gone at all as she had expected, that still made her smile. *Her* room. It was all hers. And she would enjoy it as much as possible while she was here at the Hunting Lodge.

She started down the stairs towards the servants' quarters, illuminated by several glowing bulbs affixed to sconces in the wall. Despite his insistence that the manor required no major renovations, Sir Joseph seemed to make an exception when it came to the latest innovations in technology, especially technology for home use. The kitchens had the latest range stove and oven; closets on every floor of every wing had been converted to water closets with the new flushing toilet with the pull-chains and U-bends Mrs. Avondale had always wanted installed in her own home; the washrooms had copper bathtubs that pumped water from pipes below the house and heated onsite before flowing into the tub; and of course, electric lights were everywhere.

Despite the state of the Lodge, Shirley found these innovations made the manor something of a wonder. She had never been in a house with so many modern amenities before. And according to Mrs. Preston, she could use some of them.

"Sir Joseph doesn't mind, dear," she had explained while showing Shirley around the house. "He says all these newfangled inventions he installs should benefit everyone, including the servants. But if you think those electric lights are dangerous like people say, we have plenty of candles on hand—no gas lighting, I'm afraid. Not anymore. And if you're like me and you find the idea of these modern toilets unsanitary, there are still a few outhouses behind the property, and every room has a chamber pot. Just make sure to clean the pots first thing in the morning before you start work, because no one else will."

Shirley had been amazed, grateful, and reassured by this information. She did not believe that electric lights were unhealthy for people. If anything, gas lighting led to people suffocating sometimes and candles could fall over, and she had yet to hear of either occurring with electric lights. Plus, the light was so much nicer than gas or candles. She looked forward to using them during her free moments.

The toilets, however, did concern her. The ones in London were connected to underground pipes that ferried London's waste to God knows where. These pipes were relatively new, only a few decades old, and kept the city from dumping its waste in the Thames, which had caused some bad miasmas and a few outbreaks of disease a little over forty years ago. Supposedly, the new system kept the miasmas from harming the citizens of London. However, some people claimed that those same miasmas were not only still present in the new systems, but could fly up the pipes into the new toilets and make innocent users sick.

This far from London, Shirley did not think the pipes in this house were connected to a public sewer system, but then what were they connected to? And what could travel back up the pipes if given the chance? No, she would wait a little while before she tried any of the flushing toilets.

Shirley reached her room and opened the door. Someone was sitting on the bed opposite hers.

Shirley paused and switched on the electric light by turning a knob on a dial as Mrs. Preston had shown her how to do. The figure in the second bed squinted and held up a hand as the room brightened. It was Griffin Avondale.

Shirley frowned and placed her hands on her hips. "Mr. Avondale, what are you doing here? Must I remind you that it is considered improper for an unrelated gentleman, particularly one related to my employer, to wait for me in my private room? If this is another attempt to seduce me, then I must—!"

"I'm not here for that," he interrupted. "And please don't call my sincere feelings 'seductions.' It sounds so vulgar."

"Then what are you here for?" she asked, glancing out the corner of her eye. As far as she could tell, all the other servants were in their rooms. If she needed to, she could scream and be assured of quick assistance.

"It's about Lucinda," Griffin explained. "I'm worried about her."

"Worried about her?"

"Yes. I mean, you've seen how she's been doing since...since our parents died. And I'm sure you're aware that she had an argument with Uncle Joseph. And I fear—I'm worried that—"

"That the master may send her somewhere?" she finished, thinking of the numerous discussions between Mr. and Mrs. Avondale about Lucinda's angry spells.

He shrugged. "Maybe. I'm just worried for her. And that's why I'm here. I wanted to ask if you could look out for her."

Shirley raised an eyebrow. "Me? Why me?"

"Because she's trying to convince me that all is well with her," he replied. "And I think she might be more open with you. She enjoys your company, after all."

Lucinda likes me? she thought, suppressing a snort. *News to me. She's spent quite a bit of time trying to make my life miserable. And of course she'd be more open to me. I'm a maid, after all. We're good at keeping secrets.*

Shirley considered telling Griffin "no." After all, she was no longer his or Lucinda's maid. She was Sir Joseph's, and she would already have her hands full with learning everything required to take care of this house. Griffin would not be able to compensate her for her troubles, and Shirley did not even like Lucinda.

"Fine, I will try to be there for your sister."

Griffin's face broke into a wide smile. "Thank you, Shirley!" he said, nearly gushing.

She held up a finger. "But be warned!" she said. "I am not your maid anymore; I'm Sir Joseph's. So, my duties to him go first. Understand, Mr. Avondale?"

"Yes, of course," he said quickly. "My apologies if I gave the impression that I didn't care about your duties. But thank you. You have no idea what this means to me."

Shirley only rubbed her brow, as if she were getting a headache. *Sometimes I'm much too nice for my own good*, she thought.

With an annoyed sigh, she held the door open and motioned for Griffin to leave. He pushed himself off the bed, walked past her, but paused before leaving the room. Turning to her, he said in a low voice, "Your new uniform looks lovely on you. I just wanted to let you know." And then he turned and left.

Shirley closed the door and bolted it. *What am I going to do about that man?* she wondered. *Well, he'll be off to Oxbridge in a few months. Perhaps he'll meet some lovely professor's daughter at a social event or something and start pestering her.*

Tired beyond belief, Shirley changed out of her uniform and into her nightdress. Then she switched off the light, slipped under the covers, and closed her eyes. And despite the wave of new noises that came from her new home settling down, within the space of a few minutes, Shirley was sound asleep.

Chapter Four

Wake up. Throw out any night soil you might have made in the night and clean out your chamber pot. Open the curtains for the day. Serve breakfast to the master and the siblings. Eat a quick breakfast yourself. Get the tasks for the day from Mrs. Preston. Try to get the first half of those tasks done before lunch. Serve luncheon to Lucinda and Griffin. Have a small nibble for your own luncheon. Get the other half of those tasks done. Fail to get a quarter of those tasks done or done adequately because the house is too big and there's not enough staff to accomplish everything in a single day. Sigh and move on, because, as everyone assures you, it doesn't really matter. Serve supper to the master and his family. Use whatever's left over for your own supper. Close the curtains and put out the fires. Go to bed.

Except for Sundays, when Sir Joseph took Griffin and Lucinda and the staff to church in the Closer Village, and Mondays, when laundry took up most of the staff's attention, Shirley's days took up a busy but predictable routine.

And despite the overwhelming workload, she found she liked working for the baronet, strange as he was. No matter how many of her daily chores were left unfinished or not even touched, she was never reprimanded for it, and she was still paid handsomely. The staff were kind to her, once they got over the shock of her lazy eye, and she got along well with them. Or at least, she had not rubbed the wrong way with any of them so far.

And her employer barely paid any attention to her, which in its way was a Godsend.

However, leaving her work unfinished nearly every day left her with a niggling feeling of dissatisfaction. Yes, she liked that there was no pressure on her to finish everything in a day. In fact, compared to the pressure and workload of the Avondale home, it was not just a relief but a delight.

At the same time, however, she was a maid by profession. Not only that, but she was a maid who dreamed of being a head housekeeper someday. How was she supposed to advance in her field if all she could say about her time working there was that she never finished her daily tasks?

Well, there was no point in complaining. Everyone on staff knew it was impossible to get the Hunting Lodge back to the state it had been in during Sir Joseph's father's day with only four maids. So long as she finished some of her tasks every day and the house remained in at least a habitable condition, that would have to do.

In the meantime, Shirley had other problems requiring her immediate attention. Currently, that problem was the flush toilet in front of her.

What was wrong with it? Absolutely nothing, as far as she could tell. The ceramic bowl was beautifully decorated with painted scenes of swans at play on a lake. The water in the bottom of the bowl was clean and clear. And, unlike the outhouse, there were no awful smells. There was even a basket of newspaper strips on the floor beside the base for after one had finished. Much more disposable and sanitary than the corn cobs and sticks one normally found in outhouses.

All told, there was nothing to prevent her from using the flush toilet.

So why am I so afraid of this thing? she wondered.

Shirley had been at the Hunting Lodge for nearly three weeks, but in that time, she had not used any of the flush toilets in the house even once. Which made her an outlier because, as far as Shirley could tell, everyone else used them and seemed no worse for wear. Sir Joseph used them; Griffin and Lucinda began using them after the third or fourth day; Milverton used them; the two other maids, Hilly and Beth, found them rather luxurious; and she had good reason to suspect both Garland the cook and his son used them when they needed to relieve themselves.

Only she and Mrs. Preston, who was an older and much more traditional woman than Shirley was, refused to use them. And Shirley was starting to feel silly for doing so.

However, today she had been tasked with cleaning all the water closets in the house, and she happened to need to relieve herself. Now seemed as good an opportunity as any to try out the newfangled thing.

So why am I just standing here staring at it? She knew why: because in the back of her mind, a terrifying moving picture was playing. The picture depicted the inside of the pipes connected to the flush toilet, and a black smoke rising through them, exiting into the bowl and into the washroom. The black smoke was disease and plague and death personified, and it would harm anyone who breathed it in. Like a maid standing there staring down at the ceramic bowl like it was an enemy.

Shirley shook her head. *To hell with this!* she thought, her inner voice a snarl. *You're being so childish! Just sit down and use the damn thing!*

With a huff, Shirley set down her cleaning supplies, held up the skirts of her uniform, and sat, spreading her legs over the bowl. Her knickers, made of two separate articles of clothing tied to her hips and to each other with strings and snaps, were untied and unconnected above her crotch. As she spread her legs, the gap between the two articles of clothing widened, exposing her private parts to the open toilet bowl.

Shirley shivered as she felt the cold ceramic touch her bare skin, but endured and concentrated. A moment later she felt the rush of urine inside her and heard the stream hitting the inside of the bowl. When that had passed, she squeezed the muscles in her backside. There were a few small plops and then one big plop. She exhaled.

This isn't too bad, she thought. *And it's less of a bother than the outhouses. I could see these becoming more commonplace.*

Her business finished, Shirley leaned over to grab a strip of newspaper from the basket. Below her arse, something gurgled.

Shirley froze, ears pricked for sound. When she heard nothing, she let loose the tension she had not been aware she had been holding and continued to lean over for the newspaper.

Must have been bubbles, she thought. *After all, there's water in the bowl. Perhaps when piss and shit mixes with water, it let out bubbles with a distinctive noise. I've seen enough bubbles in the shit and mud outside the Avondales' home to know bubbles sometimes appear. Perhaps I've never heard anything because I was always on the second floor.*

Another gurgle sounded from the bowl. Shirley ignored it and grabbed a strip of newspaper.

Something scraped along her arse cheek.

Shirley bolted upright with a shriek and spun around, clutching several strips of newspaper in a clenched fist. Nothing was in the bowl except her own waste. She was tempted to lean over to make sure and thankfully stopped herself. Her shit was too small for anything to hide behind, and the yellow water offered no hiding places for anything in there. She must have just imagined feeling something touching her arse. The thoughts of bad smells and miasmas rising through the pipes was making her imagine things.

But it felt so real. Like the tip of a fingernail across my skin.

With a scowl, Shirley turned around and lifted the back of her skirt. She would not look at her waste to confirm nothing was there. Instead, she would clean herself up, throw the used newspaper strips into the bowl, and flush it down. Then she would clean this water closet from top to bottom and move on. Whether or not she used a flush toilet again would be determined the next time she had to relieve herself.

Carefully wiping herself, she threw the used newspaper into the bowl and began to lower her skirt. Two large hands grabbed her arse cheeks from behind.

Shirley screamed and tried to pull herself free. In response, the hands clutched her tighter, their long fingers digging into her flesh through the fabric of her knickers. With another scream, Shirley beat on the hands holding her prisoner and pulled again. With a violent scraping of nail through cloth, she broke free from the hands' grips, stumbled forward, grabbed the washstand to steady herself, and turned around to face her attacker.

Rising out of the bowl were two long, skeletal arms, wrapped in tight, dead-looking skin. The arms reached for the ceiling, bending in places human arms weren't supposed to bend, sending piss and toilet water flying in every direction. The arms reached for her, their long fingers grasping for her face.

With another scream, Shirley ran backwards out of the water closet, stumbling and falling as she crashed through the closed door. The arms continued to reach for her, several meters long now, the hands were crawling across the floor like large, skeletal spiders.

From the bowl came a whisper in a voice Shirley recognized.

Don't grow up to be a poisoner, little girl. Or I'll come back for you someday.

"Shirley!"

"My dear girl!"

"Shirley!"

Hilly, Mrs. Preston and Lucinda appeared by her side. They all wore concerned faces as they bent down and asked her what was wrong. Shirley tried to answer, but found herself unable to speak, so instead she pointed into the water closet. All three women followed her pointing finger. After a moment, Hilly said bemusedly, "What are you pointing at?"

Stunned, Shirley looked back into the water closet. The arms and skeletal hands were gone. All the scattered piss and toilet water had disappeared. The only objects in the room were the flush toilet and the washstand.

Shirley gawped. When she finally found her voice, she whispered, "Where did they go?"

"Where did what go?" Lucinda asked.

"Did you see a spider, Shirley?" Hilly asked. "We have lots of them around here. Comes with being in an old building and all. But don't worry, you get used to them."

"Hilly, how dare you," Mrs. Preston chided. As always when in front of her employer or one of the Avondales, Mrs. Preston spoke with her Queen's English accent. "Speaking that way in front of the Young Miss is unacceptable!"

"Oops. Sorry!"

"Um..." Shirley did not know what to say. Had she just suffered a hallucination? Was she losing her mind?

No, she thought. *No, I'm not losing my mind. I can still feel where I was grabbed.*

Indeed, she could still feel where claw-like fingers had dug into her skin. Blood had not been drawn, but the indentations left by those nails still burned. Like someone had poked her several times with a hot wire. She would have to check later to make sure whatever had grabbed her had not done anything more than poke holes in her skin and undergarments.

In the meantime, there was still the quandary of how to answer the women who had come to her rescue. Should she tell them the truth? All she would have to do was show them the marks on her arse and then—what? Expect them to believe her?

If you show them your arse, they'll think you're crazy, she thought. *Even if they see the marks, they'll think you did them to yourself. You'll be out of a job and halfway to an asylum by nightfall.*

"Um...yeah, spiders," she said in a monotone. "I mean, yes ma'am. A couple of spiders startled me. They're gone now, though. Probably went through a crack in the wall."

"I did not realize you were afraid of spiders, Shirley," Lucinda commented. "But I sympathize. I'm afraid of rats, after all. Nasty little vermin."

Despite her state, Shirley had enough bite left in her to think, *I don't care what you're afraid of! I just got attacked by a pair of arms coming out of a toilet. And anyway, have you ever thought that the reason you don't know my fears is because you never bothered to get to know me? If you had, you might know I don't actually mind spiders, so long as they're not visible.*

"Are you sure you're alright, dear?" asked Mrs. Preston, helping Shirley to her feet.

She almost replied, "Yes, I'm fine," but stopped as she took in the housekeeper's face. The angle of her eyebrow, the scrunch in her forehead, the anxious line of her mouth. She was not concerned about Shirley; she was concerned about something else, though what Shirley could not say.

Deciding to err on the side of caution, Shirley coughed and said, "I'm fine. I better get back to cleaning."

Mrs. Preston still looked unsure but sighed and told Shirley to let her know if she was unwell or anything else happened before bustling off. Hilly gave some inspirational babble about working through fear before going off to tackle her own list of chores, and Lucinda merely smiled before heading back to whatever she did to occupy her time.

Alone again, Shirley reentered the water closet. Other than some black and gray dust scattered everywhere around the toilet, nothing seemed amiss. She checked the bowl and saw only her own waste and the used newspaper strips. No sign that a pair of arms had come out of the pipes and grabbed her by the arse. *If that actually happened*, a voice in her head reminded Shirley.

With an exasperated groan, she pulled the chain and watched as the contents in the bowl were sucked away with a watery roar she found a little unsettling.

As new, clean water filled the bowl, Shirley set to cleaning the room as quickly as possible. She wanted out of this water closet as quickly as possible. And given what she had experienced, she had a feeling it would be a long while before she used a water closet again.

If she ever did.

Chapter Five

Shirley entered the kitchen, where Garland and Luke were both busy placing food onto platters. Garland, a big, beefy man with slicked-back hair and tired eyes, turned around as he heard her approach. When he saw no one else, he said, "Master's spending another night in the ballroom, is he?"

Shirley nodded. Lately, Sir Joseph had been working on his machine in the laboratory through the supper hour and had been taking his meals there. This meant Milverton or one of the maids had to deliver his meal to him before joining the rest of the staff in the dining room. Tonight was the first time Shirley had been entrusted with the task of bringing Sir Joseph his meal, and she would be lying if she were to say she was not a little excited by the task. She had not been in the ballroom where Sir Joseph conducted his work as of yet, not even when Mrs. Preston had shown her around the Lodge on her first day. She was curious to see what was actually in there and why it took priority over a larger staff or doing work on the house.

With a groan of annoyance, as if the master's desire to eat alone was a personal affront to him, Garland began putting together a tray of food for Sir Joseph while his son continued cutting up the beef and placing it on a platter for the dining room. When he was done, he handed the tray to Shirley, who carried it out of the kitchen. She took each step carefully, being aware that while she needed to get to the ballroom as quickly as possible, anything she dropped could come out of her pay if it broke.

The ballroom, or laboratory as Sir Joseph preferred to call it, was at the very end of the north wing, protected by two large, oaken doors. Placing the tray down on a table underneath a painting of Sir Gregory and his sons as children, she rapped lightly on the door. "Sir Joseph?" she called. "Your supper is ready."

She waited a minute, but no response came. Thinking that maybe he had not heard her, Shirley knocked harder and repeated herself in a raised voice. The door swung inward on rusty hinges that protested loudly. Shirley leaned forward, expecting to see Sir Joseph, but only saw darkness.

No wait, that was incorrect. The room was dark, but not entirely dark. Shirley could make out low electric lights and chemicals that glowed like stars on a clear night. Shirley squinted and called out for Sir Joseph one more time. When she did not receive an answer, she shrugged, picked the tray up, and carried it in.

As expected, the rectangular ballroom was enormous, with a high ceiling and enough room that Shirley thought Griffin and his school friends might have enough space to play rugby indoors if they so desired. As big as it was though, it was also very crowded: half the room was taken up by a great edifice. Probably the machine Sir Joseph was working on, if Shirley had to guess. The other half, meanwhile, contained workbenches littered with machine parts and chemistry sets, bookshelves piled high with thick tomes and loose papers, and a writing desk covered in all sorts of papers and devices. The only thing that seemed missing from Sir Joseph's laboratory was Sir Joseph himself. Where was he?

With another shrug, Shirley carried the tray to the writing desk and placed it on the one spot not covered in papers. Task completed, she turned to leave and rejoin the other maids in the dining room. She paused mid-step, however, as she took a second look at the laboratory.

Although curiosity had been all but expelled from her nature so she could be a good maid rather than a nosy one, a wave of curiosity overtook her now. This was the first time she had ever been in an actual science laboratory and, while she had no way to know how this one differed from others of its kind, she thought it was impressive. Maybe a bit too dark and eerie for her taste, and probably not all that impressive compared to what that Edison fellow had across the sea in America.

But she felt if the impresario from Covent Garden could see this, he would give his wholehearted approval and claim Sir Joseph was part of the wave of the future or something like that.

Still, what was Sir Joseph working on, exactly? It was the one thing no one in the Lodge had a sure answer for. She had overheard Griffin try to engage Sir Joseph on his work at many suppers, but the baronet always changed the subject whenever asked. And Mrs. Preston had told Shirley on her first day that no one was sure what Sir Joseph was working on, only that he considered it of the utmost importance.

Also, gossiping about the baronet's work, while tempting, was highly discouraged among the Lodge's staff. Doing so could cost you your job, even if the staff was shorthanded.

She studied the machine from a distance, a giant mass of brass and steel taking up the far wall of the ballroom and extending halfway along each side wall. She went to take a closer look and noticed that the machine was really several machines linked together by thick wires and glass tubes. The tubes in particular interested Shirley. They looked a lot like what the impresario had used in Covent Garden during his science demonstrations. What had he called them? Oh yes, vacuum tubes. They were important in spurring the movement of trains and pumping water from the ground. Shirley wondered if these glass tubes were the same thing.

And now that she was a bit closer, she could see numbers on each machine. The one on the far right said **Number 13** in big, black letters painted on the front panel. She checked the one on the far left. Sure enough, big, black letters identified the machine as **Number 1**. She did a quick count. Six machines on each side. And the one on the far end was a single machine. That one had to be number seven, correct?

She walked to the far end of the laboratory and indeed, found a **Number 7** on the machine. If she had to guess, this one was the most important, seeing as it took up the entire back of the room. But what was this machine? What was its purpose? It had dials and switches and blinking lights like all the others, and it was connected to the other machines by wires and glass tubes like the other machines, but the only other thing that distinguished it from the other was a man-sized glass tube set in the center of its front. It looked like something one was meant to step inside and—what?

Shirley drew closer to the giant tube. She did not think this was a vacuum tube. For one thing, there was a handle and locking mechanism on the outside of the tube, and a track at the top and bottom of the glass. She was right, someone was supposed to step in and out of the machine. The only question was, why?

Shirley drew closer, hoping to find answers beyond the glass. All she found though was her reflection, and her lazy eye staring off at an odd angle. God, she hated that eye sometimes. She could never take a photograph because of it. If that eye were not marring her face, then maybe she—

"What are you doing in here?!"

Shirley screamed and spun around, hand over her heart. Standing in the doorway to the laboratory was Sir Joseph, a white lab coat upon his frame and a mask of fury upon his face. The blood drained from her face. She was in deep trouble now. Maybe out of a job.

"I said, what are you doing here?" Sir Joseph roared, striding towards her. "I do not like people lingering in here. Did you mess with anything? Did you?"

"No sir!" Shirley replied desperately, her heart beating wildly in her chest. "I-I just came to deliver your dinner, and I-I saw your machine and was fascinated. I mean, I thought those glass tubes might be vacuum tubes and I—oh please, don't fire me, sir! I promise, I'll never come in here again!"

Sir Joseph stopped in mid-stride, an odd look on his face. "What did you say?"

"Um, I came to deliver your dinner—"

"No, not that! What did you think the glass tubes were?"

"V-Vacuum tubes, sir," Shirley answered, flinching. "They've had all the air sucked out of them, right? A-And you can move things through them or have them float without crashing and breaking against the sides. Is-is that right?"

She waited, expecting to be dismissed and exiled from the Lodge in disgrace. To her surprise, however, a small smile appeared on the baronet's face. "Yes," he said, his voice barely above a whisper. "Yes, I suppose that is right. To be precise, the pressure from a lack of atmosphere pulls objects in all directions, which means they move in no direction. This keeps them from contacting the sides of the tube and giving them the appearance of floating. By creating a space for the vacuum to go, you can move the objects within the vacuum one way or another. Tell me Shirley, do you know much about science?"

"Um..." She was uncertain what to say. What would ensure she kept her job? A response popped into her mind and escaped her lips before if she could decide if it was the correct one. "Not as much as I would like, sir."

For a moment, she was sure she would be fired. After all, it was considered bad for a woman, let alone a woman of her low standing, to show too much interest in academic subjects, including the sciences. It was even said to be unhealthy and could cause issues of the mind and the womb. What if Sir Joseph thought she was mentally unwell?

But then his smile grew a little wider. "Yes, I'm sure you haven't been given many opportunities to learn science," he mused aloud. "A pity. I'm of the opinion that all mankind, including women, could and should learn from and use science to improve themselves."

All that Shirley was sure of was that Sir Joseph was delighted by her curiosity and was not going to put her out on the street. In fact, he seemed to welcome her interest in his work! Maybe she should use that to her advantage.

"I saw a man demonstrating scientific instruments and tools in Covent Garden not too long ago. That's where I learned about vacuum tubes. What he demonstrated was quite impressive. I would have stayed for more, but I had duties to perform and was expected back at home."

Good. Demonstrate that she was interested in the sciences, which was not untrue so long as they helped her, and then emphasize that she took her job seriously. This would satisfy Sir Joseph's interest in her interest, while at the same time reassure him that she was a reliable maid who put duty before pleasure.

However, Sir Joseph seemed entirely uninterested in her reliability as a maid. "Yes, I bet it was quite impressive!" he said in a raised voice, closing the distance between them and leaning in close to her. "Especially to the untrained eye. But still, anything that births in the public an interest in the sciences serves the common good, in my opinion. Oh, how lucky you were to be there to see this demonstration!"

Shirley took a step back, frightened. Her tactic had failed miserably and Sir Joseph was gazing at her with eyes that, while not suggesting madness, had an obsessive quality about them. She had seen eyes like that on Nellie's face when she was allowed to speak on the topic of cooking for too long. Only Sir Joseph's eyes were much more ardent than Nellie's, and his closeness made them appear bigger than they were.

Quickly, Shirley searched for a new topic, and went with the only one she could think of. "Er, if you don't mind me asking, sir, what does your machine do? It must be especially important for you to spend so much time on it."

To her relief, Sir Joseph leaned away from her, a joyful, warm smile on his face. "It's called the Eden Engine," he answered. "And yes, it is quite important. Let me ask you, are you familiar with the Theory of Forms?"

Shirley's stomach dropped to her feet. Now he wanted to discuss academic subjects, when she considered herself lucky for just knowing how to read and write! Should she lie? No, he would see the lie on her face. But if she told the truth, would he be upset again?

She struggled with herself and then, sure the truth would doom her, shook her head. Sir Joseph crossed the ballroom to his writing desk, gesturing for her to follow. She joined him as he handed her a piece of paper and a pencil. She glanced at the page. It was entirely blank.

"Try drawing a person," he instructed, boyish excitement in his eyes. "Doesn't have to be exact or anyone in particular. Just do your best to draw one. Any person. Just the idea of a person."

The idea of a person? An image appeared in her head, a generic man in simple clothes. If she had passed him on a London street, Shirley would not have noticed him at all. She glanced at Sir Joseph, received his nod of encouragement, and began to draw. What resulted was not anything like the image in her head. It was a simple stick figure, with sausage-like appendages for fingers and an egg with grass growing out of the top to suggest a head and hair. If the Theory of Forms had anything to do with drawing ability, she had failed spectacularly.

Sir Joseph, on the other hand, seemed pleased by her drawing.

"Let me guess," he said. "That wasn't anything like what you imagined in your head?"

She nodded.

He pointed at her. "But you can still imagine the idea of a person, right? You know without needing to be told what a person is supposed to look like. Their proportions, their facial features, the number of fingers and toes on each hand and foot. In other words, you know the idea of a person. And you know the idea of a tree as well, or the idea of an umbrella, or the idea of a ship, correct? You know exactly what they are, how they function, and what their uses are if they have any."

"Um, I suppose so, sir."

"But when you try to produce that idea in reality, it rarely is as perfect as the idea in your head," Sir Joseph explained, pointing at

Shirley's stick drawing. "And that is the essence of the Theory of Forms. The idea of something is the truer, purer version of something, and the reality is only a pale imitation or reproduction."

Shirley glanced from the drawing to Sir Joseph and back again. She thought she understood what he was talking about. "So, it's like how Mrs. Avondale and Miss Lucinda had a piece of music in their heads, but they had to work really hard to make it sound anything like it should when they attempted to play it on the piano?" she asked slowly. "Or like how I know what a peach looks like, but when I went to buy them at Covent Garden, some of them came in odd shapes not normal for peaches?"

"Exactly Shirley!" Sir Joseph's grin was so wide, it nearly reached his ears. "Very good, you've grasped the concept. And that's where the Eden Engine comes in. You see, according to the Theory of Forms, there is a place where the ideas of things, their Pure Forms, if you will, exist and are as real and tangible as you or me. The Eden Engine relies on fringe sciences, sciences not acknowledged yet by mainstream scientists such as those belonging to the Royal Society, to tap into the Pure World and bring its energy into our imperfect world. I believe if one can harness that energy, one can fix the faults in our world. The chamber you were standing in front of?" He pointed at the glass tube. "That is the bombardment chamber. If a living being were to stand in the energy chamber, they would be bombarded by Pure World energy, and any flaws they had—any diseases, any birth defects, anything that would keep them from being a perfect human being—would be eradicated from them. They would be pure."

Shirley gazed at the central machine, considering what he was claiming it could do. If what he said was possible...

"If what you say is possible, it could change the world," she said aloud. "It could end disease. Nobody would get sick anymore. Nobody would be lame or blind or deaf. Perhaps it could even end drunkenness, or stop men from beating their wives." A memory played at the back of her mind, that of a voice she didn't like to think about. *Don't grow up to be a poisoner, little girl. Or I'll come back for you someday.* "It could even stop insanity or keep people from murdering each other."

It could fix my eye, she thought.

"You are quick to understand the theory and its implications."

Shirley turned to Sir Joseph. For half a moment, she had forgotten he was still standing there.

"Yes, it's quite possible the Engine could do all that," he continued, gazing at the machine with the eyes of a proud parent. "It's still in the early phases, but I believe that by year's end, we could be seeing the greatest revolution in history as well as science. The end of humanity's impurity, and the beginning of finding their perfection." Then his eyes traveled to Shirley's. "How would you like to help me finish the project?"

Shirley blinked, surprised. She opened and closed her mouth several times before finding her voice. "I'm sorry?"

"Would you like to help me with the Eden Engine?" he rephrased. "Be my assistant instead of a measly maid-of-all-work? I'm at the point of development where I will be needing assistance anyway, and I would prefer someone I know who not only understands what I'm trying to accomplish here but shares my enthusiasm as you so clearly do."

Shirley's mind reeled. Work as his assistant? Was that even something she could do? No, she was a maid, not a scientist. She simply was not suited to work in a laboratory, no matter what the aim of the project was or her enthusiasm for it. It would be best for her to politely turn him down and hope he did not fire her in revenge.

"I'm sorry, sir," she said, carefully choosing her words, "but I am a woman and a maid. I cannot possibly help you. Besides, your staff would be in a bind if I were to leave them to help you in the laboratory."

"I can hire another maid if they're so desperate for one," Sir Joseph replied, waving a dismissive hand at her. "And as for whether a woman should be a scientist, there are quite a few women contributing to the field of science today, and they seem no worse for it. Ada Lovelace, for one. So, won't you join me?"

Shirley realized with a chill that Sir Joseph was not going to let her turn him down. One way or another, she was going to work with him on this Engine. She gulped and cleared her throat. "I-I would be honored to work with you, Sir Joseph."

"Excellent!" he cried, extending a hand to her. It took her a second to realize she was supposed to shake it, and another second to actually do so. His hand was firm and strong as it swallowed her. When he let go, he turned to the writing desk and began writing on a blank piece of paper. "We will need to get you a whole new wardrobe. After all, a maid's uniform has no place in a laboratory. I'll have a tailor come up from London to make you a whole new set of dresses befitting your new station. The one in the village can make your lab coat and boilersuits. Also, do you require anything special such as glasses to read? No? Excellent! We should also get you some scientific texts. I want you to study them as if your life depended on it. Since you will be working with me, a basic understanding of science is a necessity. And finally, you should be moved into an actual bedroom, not one of those closets in the basement. Perhaps one of the empty bedrooms on the second floor? Yes, that should do. I'll have Mrs. Preston move your things immediately."

Shirley's mind swam as Sir Joseph continued to rattle off all the things she would require as his assistant. A lab coat and boilersuits? A whole new wardrobe of dresses? A new bedroom? Her dream of becoming a head housekeeper was quickly dissipating like smoke from a flame. Once she became a scientist, there would be no going back. No one would hire her for housekeeping if they thought she was too intellectual for the work.

She grabbed the edge of the desk to steady herself. Sir Joseph failed to notice, instead turning to go and find Mrs. Preston or Milverton. Left alone, Shirley gazed at the machine—the Eden Engine, as Sir

Joseph called it. An odd sense of calm came over her as she considered the bombardment chamber, the place where transformation would happen and impurities would be removed.

Well, maybe it won't be so bad, she thought. *Not being a maid anymore, I mean. Perhaps I'll become a legend among scientists for assisting Sir Joseph. He did say this machine could revolutionize both science and history.*

Her hand went up to her lazy eye. *And maybe this thing will become normal as well. Perhaps I will become...*

She stopped herself from thinking the word "beautiful." Instead she thought, *Perhaps I will become someone people will be proud to know.*

Sir Joseph's dinner was getting cold. She decided when he returned, she would remind him of it, her last act as a maid before changing careers. She turned towards the door and waited, not realizing just how much her life would change from this moment onwards.

Chapter Six

Shirley could feel them glaring at her every time she passed them in the hallway. Hilly and Beth. Milverton. Garland and his son, Luke. Even Mrs. Preston did nothing to hide her animosity. They were all angry with Shirley, even though it was not her fault. After all, Sir Joseph had insisted she become his assistant and would not take "no" for an answer. How was she supposed to refuse and keep her place at the Hunting Lodge?

Not that they would believe her if she told them that. Not when she now wore nice new dresses from a tailor in London, functional and demure but still new and much more expensive than what a maid should be able to afford. Not when she had had her belongings moved into a large bedroom in the north wing with her own feather bed and a closet bigger than her old room. Not when she now took her meals at the dining table with Sir Joseph, Griffin and Lucinda, the latter two treating her promotion and its side benefits with confusion and perhaps a little suspicion. And especially not when her annual salary had increased so much that she only made slightly less than Milverton or Mrs. Preston did.

To the staff, Shirley was nothing more than a traitor who had left them all in the lurch so she could move her social status farther up than any young maid-of-all-work had ever gone before. And Shirley would not be surprised if they believed she had moved up while lying on her back and with her legs spread wide open. She would be angry, of course, but not surprised. Such an allegation would be patently ridiculous, of course. Only Griffin looked at her that way, and she half-suspected he only did that because she used to be a maid and not too young. Either that, or he was mad.

Still, how was she supposed to convey all this to her former coworkers when they held such resentment towards her?

The answer was, she could not, and therefore she did not bother trying. Instead, Shirley dove headlong into her new occupation as Sir Joseph's lab assistant. Which, to her relief, was not heavily reliant on knowing scientific terminology or being able to discuss the nuances of what Sir Joseph was endeavoring to do. Instead, Shirley's job consisted mainly of mixing chemicals, writing down numbers from the various dials and gauges on the machines—consoles, as Sir Joseph called them—and squeezing behind or inside the consoles to adjust or add new pieces to the machinery. It was time-consuming and physically demanding work, often requiring Shirley to arrive at the laboratory before dawn and staying until well after the sun had set. But then again, she had had a similar schedule and physically demanding job as a maid, so it was not too much of an adjustment. She had only traded in her duster and apron for a wrench and a boilersuit.

Even after she retired to her bedroom for the evening, however, her work did not cease. Rather, once she had cleaned herself up and changed into a nightgown, she would take one of the books Sir Joseph had procured for her and study the sciences. And while some of the concepts did go over her head, she found the reading fascinating. Many types of scientific study existed, for example: biology, chemistry, physics, and engineering, just to name a few. Though each was different in its way, however, they all relied on a method for testing and proving hypotheses, a method called the Socratic method. This method used trial and error to draw data and facts to either support a hypothesis, thereby transforming it into a theory, or invalidate it, thereby leading to new hypotheses and theories. Through this method, science could divine smaller details about the world, and then put these details together to form a larger picture, like pieces in a puzzle.

Shirley consumed this knowledge, eager to be of more use in her new position, and eager to understand what Sir Joseph would say when he finally explained to her how the Engine reached the Pure World and took its energy. More than that, however, she was just eager to know.

While the circumstances of her life had kept her from even thinking about science, now her duties revolved around the field and she found herself passionate for it. Indeed, she was starting to understand how Nellie felt about cooking. When you found something you were truly passionate about, you looked forward to spending your time on it, and enjoyed every moment you were wrapped up in it.

Along with the sciences, Shirley also studied the Theory of Forms, using a primer Sir Joseph had written himself. She had read that booklet front to back several times, growing more familiar with the theory each time. A theory that was, to her surprise, a philosophical one rather than a scientific one, but, according to Sir Joseph, it would become a scientific theory if the Eden Engine worked as it should.

Working by day, studying by night. Such had been her life in the month since Sir Joseph had promoted her.

That is, until one day, when she had been dismissed from her duties a bit earlier than usual.

Sometimes that happened: Sir Joseph would want some time alone in the laboratory to research or write, and he would let Shirley retire early. Shirley never minded. She could use the time to study more, or if she was let go very early, indulge in the luxury of a stroll to the Closer Village. Once or twice, she even went shopping there.

Today was another such day. Sir Joseph had dismissed her for the day and Shirley was looking forward to her free time. She had not even had a chance to decide what she would do with her afternoon, however, when she was accosted by a familiar and rather unwelcome face.

"Shirley!" Lucinda called, practically bouncing down the hallway to her. "Shirley!"

Suppressing a groan of dismay, Shirley plastered on a smile and said, "What can I do for you, Miss Lucinda?"

"Oh, do call me Lucinda," the girl replied as she bounced to a stop in front of Shirley. "You're not my servant anymore, after all. Or Uncle Joseph's, for that matter. In fact, now that we're of a closer social standing, we should consider ourselves friends!" She crinkled her nose. "Oh goodness, what have you been doing down in that laboratory of his? You stink horribly."

Shirley, aware of her unladylike smell, sighed. For some reason she had not yet received, the Eden Engine tended to give off tremendous amounts of heat even when it sat idle. This explained why, on their first day at the Hunting Lodge, one of the chimneys on the north side had not been belching smoke. The machine warmed the far end of the north wing all on its own. However, that heat tended to leave Shirley drenched in sweat, especially on warmer days like today. And Sir Joseph, afraid that someone might come by and spy on his work, refused to open a window to cool the room down, which further compounded Shirley's sweat problem.

No, not "sweat problem." "Glistening problem." Shirley may not be a lady, but she was of a higher standing now. And ladies and women of good standing did not sweat, but glisten. It was another change Shirley had to get used to now that she was a lab assistant instead of a maid.

But enough about that. Lucinda was expecting an answer from her. Shirley cleared her throat. "I was busy in the laboratory today. And I was about to take a bath before you arrived—"

"Well, that's perfect!" Lucinda interjected, her eyes lighting up like the electric lights on the walls. "You go wash up and then join me in the kitchen at half-past-nine this evening. And I won't take no for an answer!"

And with that, she bounced off, leaving Shirley agape. *What the hell does she want me to meet her in the kitchen for?*

For a moment, she considered ignoring the summons and just heading to bed after dinner this evening. Then she realized that if Lucinda wanted her to be at the kitchen at half-past-nine that badly, then it was likely the girl would wake her up and pull her out of bed if she tried to avoid the meeting. Either way, Shirley was going to be there.

With another sigh, Shirley slunk to the bathroom for a long, luxurious bath. As evening fell, she gave another sigh, put on a new dress, and headed down to the kitchen. There, she saw another familiar face. This time when she smiled, it was real.

"Good evening, Nellie Dean," she said. "Have you been invited to this evening's meeting as well?"

True to his word, Sir Joseph had found a replacement for Shirley and had her up at the Hunting Lodge within a week. The replacement, as it turned out, had been Shirley's one-time junior Nellie. Shirley had been worried the younger girl might still resent her for leaving her alone after the baronet offered her a position, but Nellie had been all smiles when Shirley had met her in the foyer on the day she arrived.

She was still all smiles as she ran over to give her one-time senior a hug. Shirley returned the hug, rolling her eyes like a good-natured older sister indulging a younger sibling. Which, in a sense, she might as well be, and glad for it. She needed a friend amongst the staff, and Nellie was the only one who had seemed genuinely happy for her when she had found out about Shirley's change in careers. Shirley would do nothing to upset that relationship if she could help it.

As Nellie let go of Shirley, she went to the cupboard and began pulling out bowls and spoons. "Yes, Miss Lucinda brought up the idea and I said I wanted to do it."

Shirley raised an eyebrow. "Do what?"

The door leading down to the cellar swung open and Lucinda walked out pushing a metal cart, upon which was a metal bucket with condensation forming on the sides and lid, as well as an oil lamp with a flame burning inside. "Goodness, it is cold down there!" she exclaimed. To Shirley, she continued, "Did you know the cellar is just one long tunnel ending in an underground cavern? It's so far underground, it stays cold year-round."

"I did. Mrs. Preston told me," Shirley replied, trying to hide her confusion. "She said Sir Joseph's grandfather had it dug that way to keep his wine cool."

"I never knew until I volunteered to get the ice cream," Lucinda revealed excitedly. "There's no electricity down there yet, so I had to take the lamp. It was a little scary, but I believe I'm now used to it. In fact, I think it's rather peaceful down there."

"You...volunteered to get the ice cream?"

"Oh, don't give me that, Shirley!" Lucinda replied. "I'm bored to death in this house and needed something to do. Now, let us enjoy some frozen treats and talk. I want to know what you've both been up to lately."

Nellie enthusiastically began helping Lucinda scoop out the ice cream and gabbing about learning to care for a big house like the Hunting Lodge. Lucinda nodded, seeming to hang on the younger girl's every word. Shirley only stared.

They're friends, she thought. *And now she's trying to make me her friend, too. And she's...doing work she'd normally ask a servant to do. Because she's bored.*

She remembered then the promise she had made to Griffin Avondale on the first night here, to keep an eye on Lucinda and see how she was doing. So far, she had not kept a word of it.

Might as well, she thought, shrugging her shoulders. *Besides, I can't remember the last time I had ice cream.*

Shirley crossed to the kitchen island and accepted a bowl of the creamy concoction from Lucinda with a polite "thank you." When Nellie and Lucinda had bowls as well, they all took a bite. As the cool, seductive treat contacted her taste buds, Shirley recognized the taste and grinned. "How did you know apricots were my favorite fruit?" she asked Lucinda.

"I didn't," she replied. "I just asked Mr. Garland to make some with anything he had handy. But I'll keep in mind that you like apricots, Shirley."

Shirley rolled her eyes but continued to dig in.

What followed was a pleasurable hour in which multiple bowls of ice cream were served and the laughter was plentiful. Nellie related some of the crazy stories involving her family back in Lambeth, which Lucinda said would make for a great Jane Austen novel. Lucinda, meanwhile, told them about an incident involving an ox and a candlemaker in the Further Village that had both Shirley and Nellie near shrieking with laughter.

And then Nellie asked Shirley what she was doing in that laboratory with Sir Joseph.

Fighting through her giggles, Shirley wiped a tear away and said, "I wish I could tell you, but I've been sworn to secrecy."

"Oh come on, Shirley!" Lucinda begged, still laughing herself. "Tell us! What is Uncle Joseph doing in there that's so important that he has to make having a ball impossible?"

"I-I'm sorry, I c-c-can't!" She burst into another round of giggling. "Did you ever notice the word 'can't' sounds kinda funny? Say it with me. Can't!"

Both Nellie and Lucinda responded with chuckles. "It sounds so...unrefined!" Lucinda replied delightedly.

"Can't!" Nellie repeated to raucous chortles. "Can't! Can't! Can't!"

All three devolved into cackles, Shirley pounding her fist against the island's surface. She had no idea why they were laughing at a simple word, but there they were.

Almost as if we're drunk.

Shirley paused, the thought repeating in her head. *Almost as if we're drunk.* Thoughts of her mother, dead nearly six years now, whirled through her head. The woman had meant well most of the time, but she had never dealt well with the vice of drink. In fact, there had been times when Shirley's mother had acted as if she needed drink. As if it were essential to survival.

Shirley had never had a drink because of her mother. In the back of her mind, she worried that if she had even a small glass of wine or beer, she would turn out like her mother, moving from rooming house to rooming house every day with a small child and doing whatever odd jobs she could to make a couple pennies to support her habit.

But there was no way she was drunk now. She had not had anything to drink.

Unless...

Shirley turned to Lucinda. "Hey Lucinda," she said, horrified to hear a slight slur in her voice, "this is just apricot ice cream, isn't it?"

Through her tears, the girl managed to choke out, "Apricot and white wine. I-I am not allowed to drink yet, so I thought this might be a good way to have some without getting in trouble."

Shirley's mouth dropped open. While she had never made ice cream herself, she knew it involved mixing cream and the flavoring ingredients together into a concoction, and then using a grinder to merge it with ice. If white wine had been added with the apricots, the alcohol would not have evaporated away as it might have if the wine had been cooked with chicken or a similar dish.

In other words, all three girls had been imbibing this evening, and only one of them had known about it.

Nellie was similarly shocked, because she was staring at her bowl with eyes as round as dinner plates. "I've been drinking," she whispered. "There goes my pledge to the Lord to never drink. What will Reverend Snow say?"

There was a pause as all three girls considered the repercussions of getting drunk off of ice cream. Then they burst out laughing. Shirley knew she should be upset. After all, given her mother's history, she had every reason to be wary of drink, as well as any food that might contain it. But good God, she could not help it! Somehow, the whole situation was hilarious!

Good Lord, is this why Mum drank? To find laughter in even the most humorless of situations? Given her life, it would not surprise me. But what will happen to me if I keep eating this ice cream? Will I end up like her? Is this something that can run in families? People talk about drunkenness like it does, but I've never bothered to find out for sure. Oh God, what is wrong with me? I need to stop now before this gets out of hand!

Before her mind could spiral any further into worry and despair, Shirley heard feet on the stairs. All three heads turned around to see Mrs. Preston arrive. "What's this, then?" she said, her Midlands accent out in full force. "Having a little party, are we? I wondered what all the noise was about."

None of them spoke. For a moment, Shirley was sure all three of them were going to be scolded, even though Lucinda was Sir Joseph's niece and Shirley no longer worked under Mrs. Preston anymore.

But then Mrs. Preston smiled and sidled up to the island. "Well, let me have some," she said. "It was so hot today, and some ice cream will do me some good."

All three of the younger girls glanced at each other before Nellie pulled out a fourth bowl and spoon and Lucinda scooped her a generous portion. Before Shirley could warn the older woman, Mrs. Preston was devouring the dessert as if she had not eaten in months. A few minutes later, she was wildly laughing with the rest of them as she recounted her own funny tales of growing up in Staffordshire.

It would seem Mrs. Preston can't hold her liquor, Shirley observed as Lucinda served the housekeeper another bowl. Having cut herself off, she was starting to wonder how she would extricate herself from this little drinking party.

Her thoughts were interrupted, however, as Mrs. Preston turned to her and said, "So, how's it working for the master, dear?"

"Um...fine," Shirley replied. "Nothing to complain about, Mrs. Preston."

"She won't tell us a thing about what she does with him in there," Nellie remarked. "We've been trying to get her to speak, but she just refuses."

Mrs. Preston, leading another spoonful of ice cream to her mouth, muttered, "Oh, it's something to do with the imperfections of man."

If Shirley had been holding a glass in her hand, she was sure she would have broken it in her grip. She had been *commanded* by Sir Joseph not to speak of the Eden Engine or his work with the Theory of Forms until he was ready to present his findings to the Royal Society. And Mrs. Preston had spoken about it as casually as if commenting on the weather. And after assuring Shirley that she had no idea what Sir Joseph was working on, no less!

"The imperfections of man?" Lucinda repeated, eyebrow raised. "What does that mean?"

Mrs. Preston finished her ice cream and burped quietly. "Excuse me. Well, I probably shouldn't tell you this," she answered, a mischievous look in her eyes, "but it has a lot to do with the master's life and his dealings with other people."

All four of them leaned closer over the island as Mrs. Preston's voice dropped to a near-whisper. Even Shirley, who had enough sense left to realize this was not a conversation any of them should be having, was curious.

"For one thing, Sir Joseph didn't have the best relationship with his parents," Mrs. Preston revealed. "Not surprising: Sir Gregory was a tough father to have at times. Oh, he could be the life of the party, and he loved riding and hunting. And he loved this house and its staff, believe me. But he was only the second baronet of the House of Hunting, and his father had only come by the title when Sir Gregory was already in his twenties. To be a new baronet, just one degree away from nobility, and among all these other established houses, is a rough lot to be dealt. Sir Gregory was aware some of his peers looked down on him as being too new for their like.

"As a result, Sir Gregory pushed the master rather hard to be the ideal gentleman. You know, strong and powerful, always aware of etiquette, knowing when to display emotions and when to bottle them up, how much to eat of any dish to show he liked the dish but wasn't a glutton. It probably hurt Sir Joseph that his father was so strict with him. He may have never felt good enough for his father, no matter how hard he tried.

"And then there was Lady Agnes. She was a lovely woman, but I'm afraid she didn't have much of a mothering side to her. She could be cold to her sons and didn't spend enough time with them. I'm sure you children understand that."

All three girls nodded, though Shirley was unsure if Nellie really understood, and was certain Lucinda did not. Having had issues with her own mother, however, she could sympathize with Sir Joseph.

Mrs. Preston continued with her story. "I thought things might improve once he went off to Harrow and then to university in London, but he didn't get on with most of the other students or teachers there. Don't ask me the specifics, I don't know. All I can tell you is, when he came home to stay after receiving his diploma, he was jaded with people and wanted nothing to do with them.

"But of course, he was forced to attend events and be part of society. Sir Gregory would not hear of his heir refusing to be social! So, he went to balls and garden parties and the like. Even hosted a few here, though he never seemed that happy at them. And at one of these events, he met Lady Wilhelmina. Wasn't long before the papers were announcing their engagement and the banns were being read."

"Was it a whirlwind romance, like they say in the novels?" Lucinda asked, sighing in that way young women do when imagining love and marriage.

"Oh heavens no, Miss Lucinda!" Mrs. Preston balked. "They hated each other with a passion. Couldn't stand each other! But things were different back then. Parents often had to be consulted if a couple wanted to marry. Some parents even made the arrangements for the children and did not care what their sons and daughters said. And in this case, Sir Gregory and Lady Wilhelmina's parents wanted them to marry. From their perspective, the two were a good match. Sir Joseph had his title and Lady Wilhelmina had her family's business assets." She paused, then added, "You know, now that I think about it, I believe Lady Wilhelmina wanted to marry someone else. She had to reject him, however. The lad was poor and had no means to support her. He would have been a poor suitor, indeed."

Both Nellie and Lucinda had crushed expressions on their faces. Shirley, whose views on marriage were more practical, felt only pity for Lady Wilhelmina and the man she had loved.

"In any case, they married. And as I said, they couldn't stand each other. They ended up having several affairs. Oh, don't look so scandalized! Yes, Lady Wilhelmina was bringing shame to both her new family and the family she'd left, but she was lonely! Her husband didn't love her, and I don't think she was very happy in a house full of strangers. Sure, she could've done more to hide them like Sir Joseph did—we weren't aware that his trips to London were to see other women until well after Lady Wilhelmina's passing—but she was lonely. We should have sympathy for her."

"Wait a minute," Shirley interrupted. "You just said Lady Wilhelmina wasn't careful with her affairs. Does that mean you know whom some of Lady Wilhelmina's lovers were, then?"

Nellie and Lucinda gasped as they realized Shirley's implication. Mrs. Preston nodded. "Three of them, to be exact. But I won't tell. After all, the poor woman has been dead for over twenty years now. Why wake sleeping dogs?"

"Didn't Sir Joseph and his wife try to get along?" Nellie asked, in a tone of voice that hinted that the survival of all her romantic notions rested on Mrs. Preston's answer.

"They did. Enough to produce a son and a daughter. But young Wesley was born deformed. Yes, you heard me right, he was deformed, both in body and mind. Sweet as a lamb and as affectionate as a puppy, but still deformed. Died at fourteen with a face as ugly as a horse's arse, and with the vocabulary of a small child. Some sort of fit if I remember correctly. He had a lot of those as he got older, though I'm not sure why."

Hearing Mrs. Preston talk about Sir Joseph's son in such a way made Shirley feel self-conscious about her own eye. She had to stop herself from reaching up to touch it—or did she want to hide it?—as Mrs. Preston ploughed on with her reminiscences.

"But then there was young Miss Emily. Oh, she was a sweet girl, and quite pretty as well. A proper lady if ever there was one. We all thought she would marry up into the highest reaches of the peerage. She was set to make her debut in society the summer after she turned seventeen. However, she died before that could pass."

"What happened?" Nellie asked.

Mrs. Preston shrugged. "No one's really sure. Lady Wilhelmina took Miss Emily to the seaside in Devon for a couple of weeks. Nothing unusual, many families holiday there. However, when she got back, poor Miss Emily started to feel unwell. Within a few days she was bedridden with a fever and then...and then after a week, she fell asleep and never woke up. Coma, is what the doctor said. Nothing could be done."

She sighed. "After that, Lady Wilhelmina became rather melancholy. And I don't mean the normal rituals of grief, wearing black and retiring from society for a time. I mean, her behavior became rather disturbing. Talking about killing herself or of hearing Miss Emily's spirit calling out to her, telling her mother she was lonely. Sir Joseph was considering having a doctor look at her.

"But before he could do anything..." Mrs. Preston sniffed, and tears welled in her eyes. "I'm not sure exactly what happened. Nobody is, really. All anyone knows is, she was in a bad state. Lady Wilhelmina loved her children, but she especially loved Miss Emily, and her death hit her hard. So, when she fell from the library on the third floor—"

Nellie and Lucinda gasped in horror. Even Shirley stiffened.

Mrs. Preston nodded, as if she understood. "I should let you girls know, there's no proof she took her own life. Even the coroner was unsure of that. Not to mention, it was hot that day, and she may have opened the windows to get a breeze. But whatever happened, it was probably a relief to the poor woman. Life had been so cruel to her. An unloving husband, one of her children born feeble, and both taken from her within a few years of each other. I'm sure the moment her soul was released from her body, the Lord took her into his arms and told her He would no longer allow any pain or suffering to reach her. Yes, that's what I believe."

For a moment, nothing was said. The kitchen was so silent, Shirley was sure she would hear a pin if it dropped. Finally, Mrs. Preston sighed again and spoke with an air of finality. "In any case, I believe this is why Sir Joseph is working on finding the cure for mankind's imperfections. Everyone in his life have either failed him or left him. 'Imperfect bodies and imperfect souls,' I heard him describe it once. 'All of man is afflicted with imperfect bodies and imperfect souls.' And so he's toiling away upstairs to fix mankind.

"Of course, that's a problem mankind alone can't fix. I'm sure any number of priests and ministers wiser than me could tell him he's chasing after windmills. Mankind is imperfect because of Eve's folly in the Garden of Eden, that's a fact. The only way we can make ourselves perfect is by following the Law of the Lord and being kinder to the less fortunate, but he still thinks he can fix the human race. And I fear he'll work himself to death in that lab of his before he achieves his goal.

"Now, you all should be in bed!" Mrs. Preston's mood, as well as her accent, changed from melancholic to proper in a second, startling all three young women. "Miss Lucinda, I'll escort you to bed right this instant. It isn't proper for a young lady of your upbringing to be up this late. You will not do so well in the morning otherwise. Nellie and Shirley—no wait, only Nellie. I'm sorry, Shirley. And I'm sorry for being so horrid to you lately. You really do not deserve it—Nellie, clean this up and return that ice cream to the cellar. Understood?"

"Yes ma'am," Nellie replied, nodding.

With an annoyed sigh, Lucinda pushed her bowl away from her. "I guess that's the end of our fun tonight," she said.

"Let's do it again sometime," Nellie suggested.

Mrs. Preston made an objection about decorum, even as she swayed while walking around the island to reach Lucinda. Lucinda, meanwhile, did not seem to care a fig about decorum, because she gave both Nellie and Shirley a hug, much to Shirley's surprise, and wished them a good night before she and Mrs. Preston tottered up the stairs and out of sight.

Despite having been exempt from Mrs. Preston's order, Shirley came around the island to help Nellie with the cleanup. She no longer felt drunk. Just unsettled. Thoughts of Mrs. Preston's story around Sir Joseph swirled through her head. Not even Mrs. Preston finally apologizing for ostracizing her this past month could fix her mood. Cleaning would help her feel settled again. Cleaning always helped her feel settled. Usually, anyway.

And I hope Mrs. Preston's wrong, she thought. *About Sir Joseph's work being folly. I think it could really help people. I could really help people. Together, with the Eden Engine, we will make humankind better.*

Chapter Seven

Some of the vacuum tubes had shattered. Shirley and Sir Joseph had discovered this unfortunate fact upon returning from supper one evening, intending to continue with some tests on Console Three before ending the day's work. They rushed to Consoles One and Two, the nearest consoles with broken tubes, examining the sparkling mess on the floor. Shirley bent down to pick up one of the larger shards of glass, holding it as gingerly as she might hold a scorpion by the tail.

"What happened in here?" she asked aloud, turning the shard around so that the low light caught it from different angles.

"Sabotage, if I had to guess," Sir Joseph rumbled from behind her. Even without looking at him, she could sense how angry the baronet was. "If I find out who it was, they'll rue the day they came in here!"

"You don't think it was one of the staff, do you?" she asked, putting the shard down. "Or Mr. and Miss Avondale?"

Sir Joseph thought about it for a moment before responding. "I'm nothing like the Sherlock Holmes fellow from the stories in *The Strand*, but I don't think they're likely candidates," he answered, his voice calmer. "We saw all of them at supper, and even the ones who had to step out for a minute couldn't have done all this in the time they were gone. Even if they had, none of them looked like they'd exerted themselves causing destruction."

Shirley breathed a sigh of relief. She may not have been a maid anymore and most of the staff continued to treat her coldly, but she still felt a certain camaraderie with them. When she had heard Sir Joseph jump immediately to sabotage, she had noticed the irrationality of the accusation and had feared for her comrades' positions. The help, after all, were always blamed for anything broken or missing within the confines of the house.

Her relief turned to unease, however, as Sir Joseph continued to make his accusations of sabotage. "If I must guess, the most likely culprits are people from one of the villages. Or perhaps one of my enemies. There are plenty in the scientific and religious communities who, if they knew of my work, might want to sabotage it. Many in the former regard me as a quack, and many of the latter think of me as a necromancer or sorcerer! Either one would feel threatened if they knew about the Engine's progress! We should draw up a list and then investigate thoroughly!"

Before Shirley could ask how many people that would require (she suspected it would be in the hundreds), there was a cracking noise from deeper in the room. She and Sir Joseph froze before turning their heads, their necks making an almost-audible creaking noise. Even in the low light, they could make out a wide crack forming in one of the vacuum tubes connecting Consoles Six and Seven.

Without a word, they rushed to the giant central console as more cracks formed in the tube. Just as they arrived, the entire tube broke apart and shattered, the pieces falling to the floor in a rain of shiny pieces. At the same time, Shirley spotted a puff of dust rise into the air from where the tube had been a moment before, dissipating even as she caught sight of it.

Beside her, Sir Joseph whispered, "So that explains it."

Shirley turned to him, confused. "I'm sorry, sir," she said, "but what explains what?"

"The glass shattering!" he exclaimed, a gleam of excitement in his eyes. The same sort of gleam he had shown when he had taken Shirley on as his assistant. "It wasn't sabotage after all! This is a discovery of how to improve the Engine!" When Shirley still did not understand, he explained, "When I first began building this machine, I made two orders for glass tubes, not realizing they would be of different thicknesses when they arrived. There was a batch with thinner glass and a batch with thicker glass. I didn't think much of it at the time; I was building the Engine as I was going along, making changes as my research and experimentation demanded.

"But this!" He pointed at the pile of broken glass at their feet. "This means something! All the tubes that have shattered were from the batch of thin glass tubes!"

Shirley let Sir Joseph's revelation sink in before looking around the room, comparing the broken tubes to the intact ones. They were about even. Her mind, already beginning to think like a scientist's, was running through possibilities of what this could mean. In two seconds, she hit on one that seemed likely to her.

"The vacuum tubes carry along the energy from the Pure World," she said. "But if only the thin ones are breaking...they can't contain the energy?"

"They can't contain the energy!" Sir Joseph repeated, his eyes as bright as Christmas lights. "At least, not the amount of energy we're siphoning off. Whatever that energy is made of, it takes a thicker glass in order to contain it and funnel it through the Engine."

"So, all we need to do is replace the tubes with ones made of thicker glass—" Shirley began.

"And we'll be one step closer to completing the Engine!" Sir Joseph finished, clasping her hands. For a moment, they held each other's hands, their shared excitement overtaking all other thoughts. Then they remembered how inappropriate it was for them to be holding hands and let go, taking a step back and clearing their throats.

"Well, I'll just clean this mess up, then," said Shirley, desperate to clear the awkward atmosphere between them. "Can't leave it to just anyone, can we?"

"I suppose not," the baronet agreed. "Would you like my help?"

Shirley cocked her head in surprise. A nobleman, or someone as close to nobility as a baronet, offering to help clean when there was a willing former maid to do it? She almost said no, but recognized the look in his eyes and replied, "I would be grateful for your help. Thank you."

A comfortable hour passed in which they gathered up and disposed of most of the broken glass, shut down any machinery that was still running, and made notes so new tubes could be ordered in the morning. While they worked, very little was said. Despite how quiet it was, however, Shirley found the work somewhat pleasant. Maybe a little fun. Even Sir Joseph appeared to be enjoying himself, once Shirley showed him how to properly hold a dustpan.

By the time they were finished and she had been dismissed for the evening, Shirley was in a good mood. Sure, it would take some time to get the Eden Engine back up and running without the vacuum tubes. But they were making progress and had some ideas about what adjustments and modifications to make to the consoles in the meantime. All in all, everything was going right with Sir Joseph's—no, with *their* work.

We will make history with this device, she mused. *No matter what Mrs. Preston says.*

She entered her bedroom, feeling as light as air.

Then she switched on the lights and her eyes fell upon a note that had been left on her bedspread.

Curious, she picked it up and read the message written upon it. *When you get this, meet me in the library on the third floor.* The handwriting was unfamiliar to her. Still, it was neat and tidy, so whoever had written it had probably taken lessons in penmanship. Shirley knew Nellie's handwriting was much messier than this, and she was certain Sir Joseph could not have written this, as she had been with him all day. So, who had left it? Lucinda? Mrs. Preston, maybe?

Frowning, Shirley considered tossing the letter into the rubbish bin and being done with it. Night had fallen and her warm bed was calling to her. Still, whoever had left this note for her had gone to great lengths to speak privately with her. Whatever they wanted to discuss must be important.

With a sigh, she pocketed the note, turned out the lights and left the room, heading down the hallway to the central wing, and then taking the stairs to the third floor.

***

The third floor was small and consisted of only a narrow hallway flanked on either side by stairs leading to the second floors of both wings, as well as the two doors which led into the Lodge's library. Shirley entered from the door on the north side and inhaled the smell of paper, leather, and ink.

Surveying the room, which was kept in much better condition than the rest of the house due to how many important tomes Sir Joseph kept in this room, Shirley's eyes settled on a figure sitting in one of the window alcoves. While light did reach into those alcoves, they weren't as well-lit as the rest of the library. It was perfect for hiding your face in plain sight. Still, Shirley squinted her eyes to try to make out the library's other patron. "Were you the person who wrote this note?" she asked, pulling it out of her pocket.

The figure stood and walked into the light. "I was starting to worry you would never show up," Griffin Avondale informed her, leaning on the mahogany table dominating the center of the room. "You kept me waiting, Shirley."

"What can I do for you, Mr. Avondale?" asked Shirley, regretting that she had closed the door behind her upon entering. He was not thinking of doing *that* with her again, was he? Yes, they were alone and the nearest person was probably at the other end of the north or south wing, but she was no longer a maid! He would not dare. Unless—

"I'm here to ask about my sister," he replied. "I understand you and that other maid from London had ice cream the other night?"

"Oh!" Her cheeks reddened as she remembered that night. She was still in disbelief that she had allowed herself to get drunk! And on ice cream, no less! "Y-Yes. I mean, yes we did. Had ice cream, I mean. It was delicious."

"And how was Lucinda? Is she well?"

"Oh! Um, yes. She's fine, I guess."

Suspicious lines appeared between Griffin's eyebrows. "Is something the matter?"

Shirley struggled to come up with an answer. After all, how could she tell Griffin that his little sister had tricked them into getting drunk?

"Well," she said after a moment's hesitation, "I believe she's beginning to think of Nellie and me as friends. She certainly acts like we are."

The lines on Griffin's forehead smoothed out and a smile peeked from between his lips. "I see. All her friends are back in London, so I guess writing to them weekly was not enough for her. Obviously, she would seek companionship with women near her own age. Er, you consider Lucinda a friend, do you not, Shirley?"

The question surprised her, and she had to think for a moment before answering. "I know Nellie is fond of Lucinda. But I...Lucinda is—"

"Somewhat spoilt and entitled," Griffin finished. "I know. I lived with her before going off to Eton, after all. I can see why you would hesitate to call her a friend."

She laughed. "Well, she's improved a little. She's certainly kinder than she used to be."

They laughed together, but Shirley's mind was running through possibilities again. Were she and Lucinda friends now? Granted, the girl had been spoilt and entitled, as Griffin said, but the death of her parents had made her mature a little. These days, she treated Shirley and Nellie like equals, rather than targets to annoy and tease. However, Lucinda seemed to have forgotten her behavior from when her parents were alive, and Shirley was annoyed by that. If she was expected to be

Lucinda's friend, was she not at least owed an apology for being treated so poorly?

Also, was there not the issue of their social statuses? Lucinda was still a company president's daughter, and the great-niece of a baronet. Up until a month ago, Shirley had been a maid, and she did not think being a scientist's assistant raised her value in society that much. Perhaps being friends with Lucinda, even if she decided that's what she wanted, was too much to ask for.

Before she could consider the matter more, however, Griffin said something that she missed. "I'm sorry?" she said, clearing her throat.

"I love you, Shirley," he repeated. To her horror, he walked around the table to her, bent down on one knee and grasped her hand. "Please marry me."

"You really must stop joking about this," she said after a moment. "I mean, it can't still be funny to you, can it?"

He shook his head. "I'm serious. We should get married. If you're worried about class issues—"

"That's one concern," she replied coolly. "And may I remind you, you're a gentleman on his way up and I was a maid up until last month? This is not a romance novel, Mr. Avondale. I do not have a secret relative or inheritance that will wash away all issues of my birth. We cannot simply overcome all obstacles. Life does not work like that."

And there was her answer: if she could not marry Lucinda's brother, she could not be friends with Lucinda. Of course, it would take Griffin's antics to make her realize it! Life was funny that way sometimes. Though she would appreciate it if life made someone else the butt of its jokes once in a while.

Pulling her hand back, she turned to leave. "It is very late, Mr. Avondale," she informed him, "and I have a long day of work with the baronet tomorrow. So, if you'll excuse me—!"

"Shirley, wait!" Griffin shouted.

At that moment, one of the electric lights buzzed loudly before suddenly shattering. Shadow fell where its light had previously shown, and an acrid smell filled the room. Shirley and Griffin paused, examining the broken bulb from where they stood with narrowed eyes. For some reason, the hairs on the back of Shirley's neck were standing on end.

"That was odd," Griffin commented. "I wonder what caused that?"

Suddenly, the light next to the shattered one flared and exploded. Shirley cried out and held up her arms in a protective X. She lowered them slightly when no glass fell near her and watched as the light next to the newly shattered one flared and exploded as well. And then the next one. And then the next. One by one, the electric lamps in the library brightened and shattered, plunging the room into darkness. A darkness so heavy and complete that not even the wan light from outside could be seen.

"Shirley!" Griffin called from next to her. "Where are you?"

"I'm right here!" she said, struggling to keep her voice even. She felt cold and on edge and there was a stench in the air that she recognized. The stench of soot, alcohol, poverty and despair. What was it doing here?

"Alright, reach for my hand," he replied. She obeyed and, after a bit of fumbling in the dark, found Griffin's hand. He squeezed it tightly but not painfully and then took a step towards her. "Let's see where the door is," he said. "Can you see the light from the hall?"

Shirley whirled her head around, but no matter which direction she looked, all was dark. A cold sweat broke on her forehead, and she reached up to make sure her eyelids were still open. When she had confirmed they were, Griffin spoke again. Apparently, he had taken her silence as an answer.

"The whole Lodge may have lost power. It may be some time before power returns. Come on, then; let us see if we can find our way out."

Tugging her arm along, he led her in the direction he thought the door was in. A moment later, however, he stopped. "That's odd," he whispered.

"What is?"

"There's a wall here," he answered. "And it's...made of stone. Brick, to be specific. How? The wall should be wood paneling, and it should be several paces away from us."

Eyebrow raised, Shirley took a few steps forward, her free hand outstretched before her. When her fingers brushed solid wall, she froze. That was most certainly a brick wall. She could feel the grooves between the bricks and the chill emanating from them. Like a cold November night in Whitechapel.

She shivered, though it had nothing to do with the feel of the bricks. "I want to get out of here."

"Let's see where this wall leads."

Griffin led them along the wall, moving leftwards towards the south-wing door. Shirley stayed a few steps behind, squeezing Griffin's hand so tight she was sure she was hurting him. She did not care. A blanket of anxiety had wrapped itself around her, her heart was beating as fast as a train engine, and that awful stench, the stench of her childhood, was growing stronger by the second.

Griffin stopped. "There's a turn here," he said. A moment later, he added, "And a corner right across from it. It's like someone put a winding hallway or a maze here."

"Griffin—!"

"How is this possible? I'm sure one of my friends from Eton could tell me, a few of them were followers of Occultism and believed in all that supernatural tosh, but I never—what was that?"

As Griffin had been speaking, the sound of footfalls echoed somewhere behind them. They stopped as soon as Griffin had commented on them. For a moment, they listened for whoever had been walking behind them, but there was nothing. Or at least, Shirley didn't think there was. The blood rushing in her ears was making it hard to hear anything.

"Is someone there?" Griffin called, his voice echoing through the space. Wherever they were, it was not the library of the Hunting Lodge anymore.

For a moment, no reply came. Whether or not that was a good thing, Shirley could not tell.

Then from far away, a voice with a thick Cockney accent echoed back to them.

"Have you been good, little girl?"

Shirley's blood turned to ice. "Griffin," she whispered. "Please, get me out of here."

"Come on," he said in a low voice, leading her around the corner he had mentioned a minute ago. Whether he had sensed her own panic or felt afraid himself, he seemed to be in a bigger hurry to get out of this place than before. From behind them, the footsteps resumed, their pace quickening.

They went down another brick-lined passage, Griffin slapping the wall to his side as he led them along. After several paces, he turned left again, which should have been impossible. There should only have been wall and bookcases in that direction, and yet they were going well past where they should have been.

From behind them, the footsteps stopped. There was a distant grunt, and then they resumed, only now they were louder than they had been before. As if whoever was following them had jumped over a wall to get closer to them.

Shirley could no longer contain her panic. "Run!" she screamed.

She dashed in front of Griffin, pulling him along behind her. Behind them, their pursuer ran down a passageway towards them, stopped, and grunted again before running after them, their feet even louder than before. Shirley increased her pace, tears rolling down her cheeks as her hand slapped against the cold stone. Behind her, Griffin quickened his pace as well, pulling up alongside her and slapping his own hand against the walls. Together, they navigated their way through the twisting passage, while their pursuer shortened the distance between them every few meters or so. By now, Shirley was certain he was jumping the walls, just like he had when she had seen him both times as a child.

But how could he be here? Here, of all places? He should be locked up in Berkshire!

Left. Right. Right again. Right a third time. Left, left, right. Left, left. Right once more. There was no rhyme or reason to the layout of this maze. By now, they should have doubled back on where they started, and yet Shirley was sure they were getting farther and farther away from that place, even as he got closer and closer to them.

Another left. Another right. Down a passageway that seemed to last forever. Left again. Left once more. Then—

"Look, the exit!" Griffin shouted.

Up ahead, they could make out the edges and keyhole of a door, light spilling into the darkness and offering them the first glimmer of hope since they had first fallen into the dark. Shirley felt her heart soar as she rushed towards the door—

The footsteps were now coming from up ahead. Shirley stumbled to a stop as a form moved in front of the door, then rushed at them. *"Come here, little poisoner!"* he shouted. *"I've gotta rip you up! Come and accept your punishment!"*

Shirley screamed. Her legs had locked up, her mind had ceased to process rational thought. All she knew was terror. Terror, and the impending sense of death, about to happen in the most gruesome way imaginable.

"Shirley, come on!" Griffin ran ahead of her again, holding on tight to her hand as he pulled her along. Her legs unlocked and she stumbled after him, even as her mind screamed that they were heading for *him*, that *he* would get them. Or was she the one screaming all that out?

Ahead of them, *he* paused, probably to raise the knife Shirley knew he would be wielding. She closed her eyes and ducked her head down, waiting for the inevitable sensation of metal piercing flesh. Instead, she felt a breeze pass over her head and heard Griffin cry out in pain. They kept barreling towards the door, now not more than twenty paces ahead of them.

"Get back here!" their attacker shouted, chasing after them.

Fifteen paces. Ten paces. She didn't dare look back, even as she sensed him lifting the knife to stab her.

Griffin slammed his body into the door. It swung open and they fell out into the lit hallway, landing on their sides with cries of pain. Shirley looked up and behind them and saw him. Saw his face. That thin, angular face, those wide, watery eyes, the scraggly muttonchops and mustache shaped like a crescent moon. The hair that should have been combed neat but was now wild and windswept. He wore the same long coat she had seen him wear on both nights six years ago, and his knife was covered in fresh blood.

"Come here, girl!" he shouted. *"All poisoners should be ripped up!"*

As he reached the doorframe, Griffin kicked the door in his face. He then let go of Shirley's hand, jumped up, and planted his body in front of the door. From behind the door came a guttural scream. *"Let me out!"* he shouted, slamming his fists against the grain and twisting the doorknob. *"Let me out! I have to rip her! She's poisoning me! LET ME OUT!"*

Griffin held firm, his face strained as he kept the door closed. Shaking on the floor, Shirley could only watch as he defended her. Somewhere in the back of her mind, she knew she should help him, but her fear kept her rooted to the spot.

Then abruptly, the noise stopped. No more shouting, no more banging or doorknob jiggling. Eyebrow raised, Griffin placed an ear against the door. "I don't hear anything," he whispered.

"Don't open it," Shirley begged.

For a moment, Griffin appeared to listen to her. Then, before she could object, he stepped back and swung the door open. Shirley screamed and closed her eyes, holding her arms over her head as she waited for the knife to fall.

"What on Earth?" Griffin wondered aloud.

Shirley opened her eyes and lowered her arms. The library was back to its normal self. No darkness, no twisting labyrinth, and certainly no sign of their attacker. Pulling herself to her feet, she poked her head in and scanned the room. It was still the library, as unthreatening as ever, if now coated in a layer of black dust she did not remember being there before the darkness had fallen. The only vestige of the ordeal she and Griffin had gone through was a single broken light, its shards littered under the sconce. In fact, Shirley thought it might have been the initial bulb that had broken before the darkness had fallen.

For a moment, Shirley did not know what to say. Her mouth opened and closed several times before she found her voice again. "Did that just happen?"

"It did," Griffin replied in a grave voice. She turned to him and gasped as her eyes lay upon his arm. His shirt sleeve had been cut, and blood was seeping out of a long, thin wound. Like a knife had cut him as he had been passing by.

Shirley's insides froze again. Somehow, *he* had been here. *He* had found her. And he had tried to kill her. Just like he had promised to do six years ago, on a dark and chilly November morning. The blood-red proof was staring her right in the face.

Chapter Eight

She had to leave immediately. Get somewhere far away. Somewhere away from him. Maybe out of England itself. France or Germany, perhaps, or maybe America. They were always looking for skilled maids in America. But why stop at a maid? She could be a scientist, a lab assistant for Edison or some other researcher. She had a little experience and an aptitude for science, so it was not outside the realm of possibility, was it?

"Shirley!"

She was startled out of her thoughts as Griffin shouted her name. Had he been trying to get her attention? She looked his way and was horrified to see that he had gone deathly pale and his forehead was shimmering with sweat. "Can you help me to the kitchen? I believe Mr. Garland keeps some medical supplies down there in case his son hurts himself while cooking."

For a moment, Shirley's brain refused to process what he said. Then her eyes roved to the wound on his sleeve and the blood seeping out. Something clicked and she figured out what needed to be done. "Come on," she said, pulling his unharmed arm over her shoulders and helping Griffin down the stairs to the second floor.

I can stay long enough to help him, she thought. *Just long enough to get him patched up and make sure he will not die. But after that, I am out of here! I will go as far as the Punjab or even to China, if it'll keep me away from that monster!*

As they reached the second floor and hobbled towards the stairs to the first floor, Milverton and Lucinda appeared, coming up from the foyer, deep in what appeared to be a serious conversation. They stopped talking, however, as their eyes fell upon Shirley and Griffin, and the latter's wounded arm.

Lucinda let out an ear-piercing scream. "Griffin! What happened!"

Indeed, what had happened? How could they tell anyone what had occurred upstairs in the library? Most of it seemed too unbelievable to be repeated. And even the part that was believable, the part involving *him*, Shirley could not bring herself to say aloud. She had been forced to drudge up those memories once already tonight. Why should she have to share them now with people she scarcely tolerated?

Thankfully, Griffin answered them before she was forced to come up with an explanation. "I was in the library and one of the electric lights shattered. Not sure how, exactly, but the glass cut me."

"My word," Milverton replied. "I've never seen any of the lights do that."

Lucinda was in tears. "Is he going to die?"

From anyone else, Shirley might have been tempted to laugh. After all, it was only a cut, and not a very deep one at that. But this was Lucinda, the girl who had lost her parents just minutes after seeing them leave her childhood home for a social call.

"He'll be fine," Shirley assured the weeping girl. "But we need to get him to the kitchen. Mr. Garland has medical supplies down there. Mr. Milverton, would you please take Lucinda and call a doctor?"

Shirley had not asked anything of Milverton since being promoted to lab assistant. She had been too afraid of the contempt she might receive from the elderly man if she had. To think, a maid who had just come to be employed by him, giving him orders!

However, contempt seemed to be the last thing on the butler's mind. Instead, he nodded and ushered Lucinda back into the foyer and down the hall to the room where the telephone was located.

Meanwhile, Shirley guided Griffin to the kitchen, which had gone quiet and cold since Garland and his son had left for bed. Sitting him in a chair in the corner, she rummaged around the kitchen and the pantry before finding the medical supplies in a metal case between the stove and the wall. Pulling it out and opening it up, she grabbed a length of bandage cloth and a bottle of cheap bourbon. She then pulled out the stopper on the bourbon bottle, soaked some of the bandages, and went back to Griffin.

"This is going to sting," she warned him. She had not even finished her sentence before placing the bandages against the wound and applying pressure. Griffin hissed, but otherwise did not comment as Shirley held the soaked bandages to his wound and cleaned up the blood with the dry ones.

An awkward silence fell, and Shirley sought a way to break it. She glanced around the kitchen and said, "Lucinda's not here yet. I guess Milverton's keeping her from making a mess of things."

"Who was that man?" Griffin asked her.

Shirley froze. "What man?"

"The man who chased us in the library, or wherever the hell we were," he clarified. "You knew him, I could see it in your face."

She kept her eyes trained on his wounded arm. "I do not know him."

"Bullshit," he replied, startling her. She had never heard anything close to coarse language come from Griffin Avondale's mouth before. "Who is he?"

"I would rather not talk about it." Shirley mumbled, avoiding his eyes.

"Well, you are going to talk about it, because I was cut trying to defend you from him!"

"No!" Shirley was on the verge of tears again. She stood, ready to bolt, but Griffin grabbed her arm with his injured one and held her firm. When she stopped struggling, he gently turned her face towards him with his free hand. His expression was kind but stern.

"Shirley," he asked again, "who is he?"

He would not let her go until she told him, she could see it in his eyes. But how could she say it? How could she say the dark truth that had tormented her in the darkest corners of her mind for six whole years?

Tears fell down her cheeks as her breath caught in her throat. When she was finally able to speak again, her voice sounded alien to her own ears. "His name is Thomas Hayne Cutbush. You know him as Jack the Ripper."

Griffin's eyes went as wide as dinner plates. "Jack the Ripper?" he repeated. "As in *the* Jack the Ripper?"

"Is there any other?" she replied icily. "I saw him kill two of his victims. I saw his face. He saw mine. Yes, I'm fairly sure he's *the* Jack the Ripper."

Griffin's mouth fell open as he beheld her in a new light. Shirley was not surprised: even six years after the murders had ceased, the whisper of the man who had killed five women, and maybe many more, in the Whitechapel and Spitalfields districts of London could bring back waves of memories. Crowds of police and private citizens searching the neighborhoods for the murderer; letters published in newspapers, one of which came with what might have been a real human kidney; and of course, the bodies of those women. The poor women who had been slaughtered, their necks slashed, their bodies mutilated. Even the photos of those women on the mortuary tables, or even just the illustrations, were enough to send people into fits of terror or dead faints.

Only in Shirley's case, she had a more personal connection to the murders. Not only had she lived in the area when the murders took place, but as she had just revealed to Griffin, she had a front row seat to some of the carnage. And it had forever scarred her.

For a moment, Griffin's mouth still hung agape. Then he closed it, coughed, and said, "Tell me everything."

"Why?" she asked, suspicious. She had never pegged Griffin Avondale to be the morbidly curious type, but one could never be sure.

"Because he cut me not twenty minutes ago," Griffin replied, his eyebrow raised. "And I can tell you're terrified of him."

Well, at least he was not displaying a morbid curiosity. Shirley had to give him that. However, she was still reluctant. She had kept these memories hidden deep within herself, fighting tooth and nail to keep them deep inside her so she could live her life. The last thing she wanted was to bring them back up to the surface, let alone share them with someone.

"Shirley," said Griffin then, his tone as serious as a funeral. "I promise not to tell anyone. I just want to understand how you know Jack the Ripper and how that led to the incident upstairs."

"I do not *know* him."

"You know what I mean."

Shirley groaned. She thought for a moment, then said, "If you tell a single soul—!"

"I give you full permission to sue me for every pound I am worth and pursue any other avenues to soothe the injury I have caused you," Griffin interrupted. "Now, are you going to tell me this story or not?"

Shirley groaned again. "Fine, I'll tell you. How much do you remember reading about those days?"

"I remember most of the details," Griffin replied. "I was away at school during most of the murders, but we got the news even in Eton."

"Well, I remember quite a bit more. Back in eighty-eight, I was a little girl living with my mother in Whitechapel. My mum was a drunk, and she often drank away whatever she managed to earn by—"

"Prostitution?" Griffin guessed.

Shirley glared at him so intensely, she was certain her eyes would set him on fire if she stared any harder. Griffin flinched, which she supposed would have to do.

"My mother was many things," she growled, "but she was not a prostitute. Just because a woman is fallen does not mean she was a prostitute. I know plenty of people think they are one and the same, but they are not. Understand?"

"I'm sorry!" Griffin replied, his voice rising an octave. "I didn't mean to imply—!"

"Well, you did!" she spat. "And let me tell you something, it's a false implication! One that men and high-society ladies who know nothing about those who have had to work from birth are all too happy to make!"

Griffin flinched again, which mollified Shirley a little. She had met plenty of so-called "fallen woman," women who had either left, been driven away, or lost their homes, husbands, and children. These women would fall on hard times and have to find alternate means to get by. Some found menial or odd jobs, others begged, and yes, a few did rely on prostitution. However, most of society seemed to think that fallen women were the same thing as prostitutes, meaning that whatever happened to them was deserved.

Given that her mother was a fallen woman, and many of the women Shirley had known growing up were as well, through no fault of their own, she tended to get a little angry when people automatically assumed all women like her mother made their living through whoring. Even if some did, it was often the only way they could afford to get by. Why did they then deserve to be treated like dirt? It was something that Shirley never understood and that just made her all the angrier.

Normally, she was good at keeping this anger in check. However, tonight was like no other night and all bets were off.

"I-I'm sorry," Griffin repeated, then coughed. "I mean, please forgive me for my ignorance. You obviously know more about this than I do."

"Obviously," she replied. "And just so you know, most of the women the Ripper killed were not prostitutes. For one thing, I knew Polly Nichols. She was a drinker, but I never knew her to whore. Odd jobs or begging or pawning her things off, sure. Anything to keep out of the bloody workhouses, but never whoring. And if you look at some of the statements from people who knew the other women at their...what do you call them? People who knew the deceased talked to judges."

"Inquests?"

"Those. Anyway, people who knew most of those women said they never whored. Not that the police or the newspapers ever cared for accuracy. Once they knew where those women were from and that they were fallen women, they thought they knew everything. And so far, nobody's bothered to correct them."

"I had no idea," said Griffin. "I will have to read those inquests someday."

"Please do," said Shirley. "Anyway, my mum and I lived in Whitechapel, but we moved around a lot. By that, I mean we usually had a different place to stay every couple of days. Any place we could find a bed for the night, or on the street if we couldn't. The only places we never went were the workhouses, because—well, you know."

Griffin nodded, which impressed Shirley. Apparently, he had some idea of how the world worked outside his own social class.

"Well, when Mum was sober," she continued, "she would give me what money she managed to earn and have me get a bed at one lodging house or another. Her job was to go buy us some cheap food for dinner. Of course, most of the time she would just disappear and end up drinking at one place or another, leaving me to go out to find her and bring her back." She paused, then added, "It's because I went out searching for her that I saw the Ripper kill two women: his first victim, Polly Nichols, and his last victim, Mary Jane Kelly."

Shirley paused long enough to remember the Whitechapel of her youth—run down, desolate, full of people with hungry bellies and hollowed-out eyes—then took up the thread again.

"It was August, and well past midnight when something outside woke me up. A cat, I think. I saw that Mum hadn't come back yet, so I got up to get her. On the way out, I told the guy behind the desk I was going out and not to let my room out to anyone—though I doubt he would have let me back in if I had come back unless I paid for the room again, it was that kind of establishment—and left. I looked all over Whitechapel that night, all her usual haunts when she went drinking, and then all the unusual places. You know, places she might pass out but wake up a bit more comfortable than other drunks. Even when stone drunk, Mum knew how to find the best places to pass out.

"Around three, I ended up on Buck's Row. I was just wandering around, hoping to find her, when I heard snoring from a stable yard. The gate inside had been left unlocked, so I peeked in and saw a woman sleeping against the wall. At first, I thought it was Mum, so I went to go wake her up, but as I got closer, I saw it was Polly Nichols. She and my mum sometimes worked together to get coin. Since it wasn't Mum, I was going to leave, but then I heard the yard door open. You didn't let yourself be found by unknown people in Whitechapel at night, not even before the murders, so the moment I heard the door, I went and hid."

Shirley took another deep breath. "And that was when he showed up. Thomas Hayne Cutbush, though I didn't know his name at the time. I'd never seen him before, either. I also had no idea what he was going to do. I thought he might work at the stable yard, or maybe he was a friend of Polly's looking to bring her home. You know, like I was looking for my mother."

"Did he look like he did...you know?" Griffin tilted his chin upwards towards the library.

She nodded. "Right down to the muttonchops and mustache. And he wore that same long coat. Anyway, he went to Polly and stared at her for a while. I thought it was strange for someone to just stare at a sleeping woman like that and wondered if I should say something to him. Before I could, however, he punched her in the neck! No warning, not a sound! He just punched her! And then he did it again! He punched her twice from both sides with both fists. Polly woke up, but she was too drunk and confused to understand what was going on. She just sat there, moaning.

"Then Cutbush reached into his coat and pulled out a knife." Shirley gave Griffin a pointed glance as she said, "Do you know what the sound of a throat getting cut sounds like?"

When he shook his head, she said, "It's like the sound of shears cutting leather, followed by water gushing out of a pipe as the blood rushes from of the neck. I'll never forget that sound as long as I live. Nor will I ever forget Polly Nichols waking up to find her neck slit, or the sound she made as she noticed Cutbush standing over her with a bloody knife. Like she was trying to ask him a question, but her throat was too filled with blood to ask.

"But that wasn't the end. Before she could properly die, he pulled her by the hair so she lay on the ground, sat on her, and started stabbing her! Over and over and over! Plunging the knife into Polly with such anger, such *hate*, as if she had murdered his mother! Every stab shook her body, and it was so intense, Polly's skirt fell up from her ankles to her waist. I wouldn't have believed it unless I'd seen it myself.

"And after he finished stabbing her, he stood up, posed her sitting up like she was a doll, and put the knife back in his coat. Then he spoke. I didn't catch all he said, but I did hear one word clearly. 'Poisoner,' he said. Then he ran and jumped over the wall. He jumped! That wall was taller than him, but he jumped over it anyway. Up, over and out of sight, like a circus acrobat or something!"

Shirley sighed. "I didn't see him again for almost three months after that. And I thank God I was too scared to even scream when he murdered Polly, because I'm not sure I would be alive today if I had."

"What did you do afterward?" Griffin asked.

"I got out of there as soon as I was sure it was safe to do so," she replied. "Obviously! And a good thing too, because not twenty minutes later someone found the body and the whole neighborhood was filled with police. Meanwhile, I found my mother with a friend, both drunk and singing in a tavern. They took me upstairs to a room they'd rented and slept off the drink, while I stayed quiet after what I'd seen. I never even told Mum about it."

"Why? Why didn't you tell anyone?"

"Because I was scared!" Shirley answered. "I was only ten! I was afraid if I told anyone, the man with the knife would find and kill me. And besides, I didn't think anyone would believe me. Mum would say I'm making stuff up and that I couldn't possibly have seen a murder, not with my eye." She pointed to her lazy eye, nearly poking it with her vehemence. "And I'm sure the bobbies would've thought Mum was putting me up to it as well, because they would've said the same thing. I mean, who would ever want to believe a little girl with a funny eye from Whitechapel, brought in by her mother who would need a couple of pints before taking her to talk to the police!"

"But your eye doesn't keep you from seeing things," Griffin pointed out. He did not dispute the rest of her description of herself or her mother.

"Try telling that to Mum and the bobbies," Shirley scoffed. "Try telling that to everyone I've ever met. Even Nellie, as well as your mother and your sister, didn't believe I could do my job until they actually saw me at work. All people see is my eye, and they decide I must be a useless cripple! They're always so surprised when they find out I'm good at what I do."

"I see. So, what happened then?"

Shirley shrugged. "The murdered woman was identified as Polly Nichols. People talked. Some thought a gang had killed her, others pointed a finger at a Jewish bootmaker named John Pizer, who was nicknamed 'Leather Apron.' But people died all the time, and I guess they thought life would move on.

"That is, until Annie Chapman died a little over a week later, and people started talking about a murderer in Whitechapel. And then Elisabeth Stride and Catherine Eddowes were murdered on the same night. And then people started calling the murderer by a name: Jack the Ripper, after what he'd signed his name as in a letter to *The Star*."

"Do you think this Cutbush fellow wrote any of those letters?" Griffin asked.

Again, Shirley shrugged. "I don't know. It's possible. I know one of the letters that went to the Vigilance Committee had half a human organ in a box it came in, but I cannot be sure Cutbush sent them. All I know is, after Stride and Eddowes were killed, the murders suddenly stopped. And as months passed, people started hoping Jack the Ripper was done killing and tried to move on.

"By the time November rolled around, Mum and I had moved out of Whitechapel and were living in Spitalfields. Mum wanted to get away from the murders and all the fear. I think she was afraid it was having a bad effect on me. And she was not wrong: women had died and I had seen one of them die, though I kept quiet about it. And like everyone, I was scared of another murder happening, even as I wanted to think it was all over.

"But then one night I had to go out and find Mum again. She had made some friends around Miller's Court on Dorset Street, so I went there first to look for her. But I never even got that far, because as I was passing by Miller's Court, I saw *him* on the other side of the street looking out a first-floor window! No mistaking it, it was the man I'd seen kill Polly Nichols, just gazing out the window and onto the street. Then, as I recognized him and gasped in shock, he closed the curtains so nobody could see inside.

"And I knew right then, I knew there was going to be another murder.

"For a moment, I did not move. I had no idea what to do. Should I run? Go find help? Confront him? But then I heard a woman's laugh, so loud that I could hear it across the street. He was with someone! So, I crossed the street and peeked through a gap in the curtains to see who he was with. What I saw was a naked woman in a bed near a roaring fire.

And then Cutbush approached the woman. I think she was expecting him to do...well, you know. But then he pulled out the knife.

"I remember how the woman's face fell, and how she sucked in breath to scream. But before she could, Cutbush cut her throat!

"And then I screamed. I couldn't help myself. I screamed. And that was when Cutbush saw me. He turned around and saw my face through the gap in the curtains. The look of rage in his face—!" She shuddered. "I screamed 'Murder!' and tried to run, but he ran out the door to the woman's room and caught me before I'd gotten ten paces. Then he dragged me into that room and...forced me to watch." She shuddered again as tears ran down her cheeks. "He spent over an hour with her. Destroying her. Making her no longer a woman, but a—a *display*! A piece of art out of hell! Some sort of tribute to his hatred of women and his sick ideas of revenge!

"A-And I was sitting in a chair there, tied down by a ripped length of fabric from one of the woman's dresses, and gagged with more fabric! And if I tried to close my eyes or look away, he would turn around and threaten me with the knife, so I-I watched all of it. Everything he did. Every single thing."

There was silence for a while as Shirley tried to collect herself again. When she began again, her voice was steady, though she noticed a sob at the back of her throat threatening to escape, and she was sure Griffin heard it, too.

"When he was done, he was covered in blood, and he had the biggest grin on his face. Like he'd achieved something great and noble! He turned to me then, and I was sure this would be the moment when I would die, when he would stab me and make me into a display just like his other victims. Instead, he untied me from the chair, threw what remained of the dress and the pieces he'd torn off in the fire and, after making sure the coast was clear, threw me over his shoulders and carried me out of there!

"I was so shocked and scared, I didn't struggle or scream or even move. I would realize years later that he was using me as cover, pretending to be a father carrying his little girl home or some ruse like that. I'm sure if I'd fought, the jig would've been up and he would've been caught, but I was sure if I so much as twitched a finger, he would cut my throat!

"When he finally put me down, we were far from Miller's Court. We were so far away, I didn't even recognize where we were, though I don't think he knew that. He bent down in front of me so we were eye-to-eye, and said, 'I had to kill her. I had to rip her up. Do you know why, girl?'

"I shook my head, too scared to speak. 'Because she was a poisoner,' he said. 'She and her bloody kind poison men, good men like me. I'm sick because of women like her. I had to send a message to her poisoning friends. That's why she and all those other women had to die. Understand?'

"I nodded my head. I was crying and sure he would kill me, even if I agreed with everything he said. Then he smiled and said, 'Good girl. Now, you be good and don't grow up to be a poisoner. If you do, I'll come find you and rip you up.' And then he kissed my forehead! I remember feeling how cold his mouth was, the scratch of his mustache, and the smell of blood. God, that smell! It clogged my nose and made me unable to smell anything else for days!

"I pissed myself then, but I don't think he cared. Instead, he walked over to a high wall and jumped over it, leaving me there alone. I didn't move until the sun came up, and a bobby found me in the alleyway. He asked me if I was alright and if I'd been injured. I didn't know it at the time, but Cutbush had left blood on my forehead when he'd kissed me, and the bobby probably thought it was my blood.

"The bobby then smelled my piss, noticed my eye, and decided I was an idiot, because from then on he treated me like one, and would only touch me by holding a bit of fabric from my dress between two fingers. Like he thought idiocy was catching.

"Mum found me around evening. She got me out of the police station and beat me so hard for making her worry. I took it. I didn't care. I was alive. And by that time, they had found the woman he'd killed, Mary Jane Kelly, and I was so glad I did not wind up like her. Dead. Murdered by Jack the Ripper, who thought women were poisoning him.

"Ever since then, just hearing about the Ripper, or about the women he killed, is enough to give me fits. I even saw a book about the Ripper on the day your parents died, and I almost couldn't breathe! And now he's here, and I—!"

"How did you find out his name?" Griffin interrupted.

"Huh?"

"He never told you his name, did he? How did you know his name?"

"Because Cutbush was caught and put away for other crimes," Shirley explained. "I saw it in the paper three years ago. He stabbed some women in their backsides. Got sent away to an asylum in Broadmoor for it. The article I read showed a sketch of the man. I swear I nearly fainted when I read that article, because that sketch was a dead ringer for the man I saw kill Polly Nichols and Mary Jane Kelly. And right under his picture was his name. *Thomas Hayne Cutbush, 26, convicted of stabbing two women in the buttocks.* That's when I knew the Ripper's name."

She smiled a cheerless smile at Griffin. "So yes, I know who Jack the Ripper is. And you are the first person I've ever told, Griffin. Consider yourself lucky, I guess."

"Good Lord," he whispered. Then his eyes lit up. "But you can tell people now, can you not? I'm certain if you told someone now, a reporter or a policeman—!"

Shirley laughed, but her laugh was as mirthless as her smile had been. "Oh, that would be nice! To tell people about Cutbush!" She turned scornful eyes on him. "I'm not the only one who figured out who the Ripper is. A couple of months ago, *The Sun* put out a bunch of articles saying Cutbush was the Ripper all along!"

Griffin stared at her. "*The Sun* said that?" he replied, aghast. "That new newspaper Father sometimes read?"

"The one and the same," Shirley replied. "For a paper barely a year old, I guess it has some smart people on its staff, to have figured it out when no one else did. But guess what? It didn't do anything! The police responded and said there was no way Cutbush could have been the Ripper. Even Scotland Yard's Chief Inspector said it couldn't have been him!"

"Why did they say that?" Griffin asked, aghast. "How are they so sure?"

"Because his uncle's a policeman too!" Shirley revealed. "Charles Cutbush, Police Superintendent."

Griffin's face fell as her words sank in. He understood that this went beyond ordinary police corruption or incompetence. Many still said Scotland Yard had done a terrible job of chasing the Ripper and blamed the police for the murders going on as long as they had. If it was proven that a relative of a police superintendent had been the murderer this whole time, the resulting scandal would have ruined the entire police force for years to come. So, of course, they would defend the murderer. They had no choice.

"That's why I can't tell anyone else about this," Shirley said with an air of finality. "And now that you know, you should probably leave the country."

Griffin blinked. "Leave the country?"

She nodded. "It's what I'm doing. After all, now that he's here—"

"Hold on a minute! We don't know that he's here."

"He just cut you upstairs!" Shirley pointed out.

"Yes, in a dark maze that suddenly appeared in a library!" he reminded her. "Listen to me, Shirley. I have no idea what actually occurred upstairs, but I doubt we really had a visit from this Cutbush fellow. You said yourself he is locked up in Broadmoor, correct? That's over a day away on foot! If he had actually escaped Broadmoor, it would have been front page news and everyone would know his face. How could he get all the way here without anyone noticing? He certainly could not take a train!"

Shirley's train of thought crashed to a halt as she considered that possibility. "True..."

"And there's been some...other odd things happening at the Lodge," Griffin went on. "Besides the maze in the library, I mean. The other day, I—well, it doesn't matter. The point is, not everything is as it seems here, so I would say it is a little too early to be leaving the country. Let me at least make inquiries at the asylum and make sure Cutbush is still there. We should have a better understanding of the man's situation, as well as of what occurred upstairs, before we do anything drastic. Can you just wait until I have done a little investigating, Shirley?"

Shirley thought for a moment. She thought of the strange occurrence in the water closet last month, when those hands had reached out of the toilet bowl for her. She had heard Cutbush's voice then too, had she not? Was there some sort of connection? Something that did not have to do with Cutbush getting out of the asylum and coming after her? She should at least stay long enough to find a common link and come up with a theory using the Socratic method. That was what Sir Joseph, as well as the other great scientists she had become acquainted with since becoming a lab assistant, would do.

She sighed. "Fine. But if he's not there—"

"I'll grab you and Lucinda and we'll leave for America as fast as possible. We can get married on the ship if you like."

"Why are you so obsessed with marrying me?" she asked with another sigh, not in the mood at all for Griffin's antics. "What did I do to earn your ardent love and devotion?"

He smiled at her, the first smile he had given her all evening. "The first time I was home and you were working for my parents, I came up the stairs to get something from my bedroom. And there you were, cleaning my window while the sun shone down upon you. You looked like an angel right then. And when you finished and surveyed your work, you were so proud of having completed a job well done. And yes, I saw your eye. But I did not care. To me, in that moment, you were the most beautiful thing I had ever seen. And you still are."

Shirley's face became hot. She glanced away from Griffin and noticed the bandages she'd been holding to his arm had fallen to the floor. "You're obviously delirious from blood loss!" she said, going to grab fresh bandages. "Where is that doctor? I should ask him if blood loss causes madness."

Griffin began to protest that he was not mad or delirious when they heard the sound of feet on the stairs. Sir Joseph, Lucinda, Milverton, and a man Shirley assumed was the doctor burst into the kitchen. The doctor quickly went to examine Griffin, while Shirley gave a bewildered Sir Joseph the same lie she and Griffin had fed Milverton earlier that evening.

"My goodness," Sir Joseph said. "I didn't think electric lights could cause injuries like that. Not unless you fell into one, that is. I must speak with the manufacturer and get to the bottom of this before I have a new light installed. And in the meantime, Lucinda—!"

"No!" Lucinda cried petulantly. Under normal circumstances, Shirley would have rolled her eyes and thought of Lucinda as a spoiled brat. However, the anxiety and terror in the girl's eyes told Shirley what was really going through her mind. "You cannot make me! I want to stay with Griffin!"

"Do what Uncle Joseph says, Lucinda," Griffin told her. "He only means well." The look on his face suggested he did not really mean what he said, but Shirley did not think anyone else cared.

"But—!"

"Lucinda," Shirley interjected, an idea coming to her, "how about I go up and spend the night with you? That way, you will have someone to wait with until we know if Mr. Avondale is alright."

"Oh, call me Griffin!" Griffin interjected. "You were fine calling me that a moment ago, were you not?"

Lucinda perked up a little at Shirley's suggestion and allowed herself to be led out of the kitchen. On the way out, she procured promises from Milverton and Sir Joseph that they would let her know her brother's condition as soon as the doctor was done with him. Shirley said nothing, not wanting to spend another minute in the kitchen. Not after what she had confessed to Griffin and what he had then confessed to her.

And she would have to be careful not to call Griffin by his given name again. That was a slip that would not do if it happened in mixed company. Some might even allege they were having an improper relationship and point to her using his given name as proof.

As she and Lucinda made their way upstairs to the latter's bedroom, Shirley was glad for the younger girl's presence. Being there to comfort her while they awaited news of her brother's condition would be tiring for the both of them, but after the events of tonight, Shirley needed someone nearby as much as Lucinda did.

And besides, if Cutbush did appear in the halls or in Lucinda's bedroom, two women could scream louder than one, could they not?

Chapter Nine

Griffin Avondale was as good as his word: he went and made inquiries as to the whereabouts of Thomas Hayne Cutbush for Shirley. Two weeks after the incident in the library, a letter came from his family's former barrister in London, Mr. Leopold. The letter, which Griffin shared with her the very day he received it, was business-like and straight to the point:

Dear Mr. Avondale,

I investigated the matter as you asked. And while I cannot fathom why you would be interested in knowing the whereabouts and condition of a man with as strange and morbid a record as Thomas Hayne Cutbush, I will refrain from asking questions and instead report my findings.

As you expected, Mr. Cutbush has been incarcerated at Broadmoor Hospital since his sentencing three years ago and has not left the confines of the ground since. While the chief doctor was unwilling to speak with me due to legal and ethical concerns, several of the orderlies were willing to give me information on Mr. Cutbush's disposition in exchange for a few shillings. Do not feel the need to reimburse me. Rather, I would prefer it if you consider this penance for being unable to help you with your father's company after his passing.

The hospital orderlies report that Mr. Cutbush is extremely violent, and regularly threatens to attack staff and patients alike. According to several orderlies, some of his favorite expressions involve "ripping" people apart, mostly anyone he doesn't like, but especially women. He believes he's being poisoned by the hospital staff, especially the female nurses, and only by killing his poisoners can he get them to leave him alone.

However, there has been no instances of his actually causing physical harm to patients or staff and there have been no serious attempts by Mr. Cutbush to escape the facility. At this time, I would say it is fairly unlikely he will ever taste freedom again.

I hope you find this information satisfactory. Again, do not worry about reimbursing me for my services. If you ever need me for more conventional services for a man in my field, let me know and I would be more than willing to be of assistance.

Regards,

Mr. Marcus Leopold, Esq.

Leopold and Banks

London

After reading over the letter, Shirley had read it again three more times just to be sure it really said what she thought it said. "Thank you, Griffin—Mr. Avondale," she said, correcting herself quickly as the latter opened his mouth. "I appreciate you going out of your way to investigate this for me."

She expected him to smile then, but instead his face remained serious and firm. "You know this means that what we encountered in the library that night wasn't the man you met six years ago?" he reminded her. "That means there is something else going on at the Hunting Lodge."

Shirley turned away from him. "I realize."

"Then we should find out what it is. After all, whatever we encountered could very well kill us. But if we can get to the bottom of this mystery and figure out what it really was we experienced—!"

But Shirley did not want to hear anymore. She headed for the foyer, saying as she went, "If we go looking for trouble, then trouble may very well kill us. Perhaps if we leave it alone, then it will leave us alone."

Although she could not see him, she could tell just how high his eyebrows were by the surprise in his voice. "You cannot honestly mean that."

"I do," she said. "And now if you do not mind, I must head to the laboratory. Excuse me, Mr. Avondale." And with that she left, hoping to God Griffin would not chase after her or try to otherwise stop her. Fortunately, he did not.

**

It was not as if she did not care about whatever had occurred in the library. Far from it. Shirley cared quite a great deal. However, even if that had not been the real Thomas Hayne Cutbush, she did not want to go after anyone or anything that resembled him, let alone could hurt her like it had Griffin. Her terror was enough that it crushed any desire Griffin had managed to raise in her to solve the mystery regarding what had occurred in the library, as well as the water closet before that. Therefore, Shirley decided the smart thing would be to avoid such strange events, stay focused on her work with Sir Joseph, and hope she never experienced anything like it again.

Thankfully, her work with Sir Joseph was enough to occupy most of her attention. The Eden Engine was in an important stage of its development, and Sir Joseph needed her now more than ever. At the same time, Shirley was advancing with her scientific studies, advancing at a lightning pace through the works of Brahe, Kepler, Newton, Ampère, Darwin, Mendel, and so many more. At times, she felt she was becoming a human library or repository of scientific knowledge with all reading late into the night she did.

Add in that Lucinda was clinging to her more than usual and expected her and Nellie to be available at least once a week to socialize with her, Shirley's schedule was quite full. Who had time to investigate the weird but infrequent happenings at the Hunting Lodge?

More importantly, Shirley reminded herself, *it gives me an excuse to avoid Griffin Avondale.*

Avoiding Griffin Avondale was important. Ever since that night in the kitchen, when he had told her how he had first fallen in love with her, Shirley had realized that it was not lust nor obsession that had brought Griffin's attentions on her, but honest love and attraction. And that made her uncomfortable. Not because she found him repulsive, exactly, nor for her normal reasons to reject a suitor. This was an uncomfortable ache in her chest that also had the odd effect of making her face hot.

Whatever its cause, Shirley was determined to keep away from Griffin as much as possible. And for a while, it worked. She found excuses not to see Griffin outside of meals, and she kept conversation civil and polite when she was forced to speak to him.

And then the day of the surprise garden party came.

***

One evening, Shirley left the laboratory in a good mood, musing on how she would spend her first day off ever. Well, calling it a day off was being generous: the truth was, Sir Joseph had told her earlier in the week that he would be spending Saturday deep in research before their first test of the Eden Engine on a live animal. As Shirley was not yet far enough in her scientific studies to fully understand the texts Sir Joseph would be using for his research, the baronet had told her to spend the day studying by herself. So it was less of a day off and more of a day-long research marathon.

Whatever she called it, however, she was looking forward to having some time to herself. She was musing on how best to spend her study time when she saw Nellie running down the hall to her, close to tears and babbling so fast that Shirley had difficulty understanding her.

"Whoa, slow down, Nellie!" she urged, grabbing the younger girl by the shoulders. "Stop. Take a deep breath like the Indians do. Good. Now, can you tell me what has you acting like your own mum died?"

"Not my mum! Hilly's mum!" Nellie replied, tears flowing down her cheeks. "And not dead, dying! Hilly got a telegram today telling her to go home to Devon to see her before she goes. She won't be back for at least a week!"

"That's awful," Shirley said, feeling more bemused than saddened or horrified. She had no idea Hilly and Nellie were so close that the former's mother dying could upset the latter so. "You must care a lot about Hilly to cry for her mother like that."

"That's not why I'm crying!" Nellie moaned. "You see, Hilly and I were supposed to help out Saturday."

"Help out Saturday?"

"With the surprise party."

"Surprise party?"

"Lucinda's surprise party!" Nellie nearly shouted. A stricken look came over her, and she checked to make sure they were not being overheard. Then lowering her voice to a whisper, "Didn't Mr. Avondale say something to you? He was going to invite you. He thought Lucinda would be happy to have you there."

Shirley thought back on the past week. She had noticed Griffin had been trying to talk to her more than usual, but she had thought he was just especially eager to discuss either marrying her or the need to find the Cutbush-lookalike.

Apparently there was more on his mind this week, she thought. As Nellie waited for an answer, Shirley cleared her throat. "Oh yes, the surprise party! Now I remember! And...Hilly not being there is going to cause problems?"

"We're short someone to serve the refreshments and sandwiches!" Nellie insisted, jumping up and down for emphasis. "And we can't find someone at the last minute to serve at the party! Mr. Avondale had enough trouble finding servers with the right wardrobes from the villages to come!"

"Why can't he get someone from London?"

"Mr. Avondale would have to pay for a carriage to bring them up and then bring them back! He can't afford that! He's already spent so much to even make this party happen! And the Master won't pay for someone to come up from London! If we don't have enough servers—!"

"If we don't have enough servers, the guests at the party will be unable to enjoy themselves to the fullest, meaning it'll be a disaster and the Avondale's siblings will lose respect and standing in society." Shirley barely suppressed a role of her eyes as she finished Nellie's sentence. She had no idea how such a tragedy was supposed to occur, given that there would have to be a noticeable difference in service through lack of a single person. Then again, most of what occurred in upper society mystified her. "Nellie, you do know that none of my previous employers ever let me serve at dinner parties, don't you?"

"But Shirley!" Nellie begged. "We need you! Can you not do this? If not for Mr. Avondale or for me, for Lucinda? I am sure if you explain to the Master, you can get Saturday off—!"

"I already have Saturday off," Shirley interrupted. "But I'm supposed to—!"

"Fantastic!" Nellie screamed, hugging Shirley around the middle. "I'll inform Mr. Avondale that you'll be there. Remember, the party starts at noon and goes till four. Wear a white dress and an apron, and let Mrs. Preston know if you don't have a white dress. Thank you,

Shirley! You have no idea how much this means to me! Or how much it will mean to Lucinda!"

And with that, Nellie bounced away, leaving Shirley with her mouth hanging open and her arm outstretched as if to stop the young maid. She withdrew her arm and closed her mouth. *Well, I got her hopes up*, she thought. *I guess I have to deliver.*

In the end, Shirley liked Nellie more than she cared for Griffin or Lucinda Avondale and she hated to see her disappointed. Which was why, on the day she was supposed to be devoting to her studies, Shirley found herself wearing a white dress and apron, standing under a tent with Nellie, Mrs. Preston and several hires from the Closer Village to serve tea or cucumber sandwiches to guests, and trying to ignore the glances directed at her lazy eye.

Though while she had no desire to be here, she had to admit that Griffin Avondale knew how to plan a nice garden party. He had directed for everything to be set up within walking distance to the Lodge, with several round tables covered in white tablecloths arranged around a wooden platform built for dancing. Beside the platform, a quartet of musicians were serenading the guests with their instruments. Like the extra servers, they were hires from the Closer Village, though they had enough knowledge of what was considered "high class" music to please the guests.

As for the guests themselves, they were a mixed lot. Men old and young were smoking cigars and talking in small groups as they awaited their turns with an archery set; married women and older ladies walked and gossiped across the lawn; and a gaggle of young ladies around Lucinda's age were playing croquet in the shade of a large elm tree. Lucinda was, of course, among those young ladies and she had the widest smile on her face.

Shirley glanced at Nellie, who was sneaking peaks at Lucinda playing croquet with a troubled expression. The younger girl noticed

Shirley watching her, however, and quickly became engrossed with arranging the sandwiches in a neat manner.

I think I understand what she's going through, Shirley thought, glancing at the croquet game again. *Lucinda was acting like we were her only friends in the world, and now she's ignoring us to play knock-the-ball-around-with-a-mallet. Must be hard for Nellie. She really thinks Lucinda is her friend.*

Then again, it was not as if she could blame Lucinda for wanting to spend time with her society friends, either. After all, she was still technically in mourning for her parents, during which time she was not supposed to have any visitors, go visit anyone else or attend social gatherings. The only reason she was able to attend this party was because her brother was taking advantage of a loophole in the guidelines: Lucinda could attend the garden party, so long as everyone agreed that she had not attended it, let alone attended it while still wearing a black mourning dress.

And thanks to that little loophole, Griffin had been able to throw this little surprise party for his sister and relieve her of some of her boredom here at the Lodge.

Speaking of which, where was Griffin? Shirley scanned the crowd and spotted him talking to a young lady in a bright red dress who had previously been playing croquet with Lucinda and her cohorts. Shirley glanced at the croquet game and noticed all the players had ceased play. Instead, they were watching their friend talk to Griffin with the utmost interest. She glanced back at Griffin and the young lady and noticed the way the latter held herself, as well as the tilt of her head.

Oh, so that's how it is? she thought, scoping out how Griffin was reacting. He seemed quite aware of what this young lady wanted from him and was flattered. Maybe even enjoyed the attention a little.

I should have known, Shirley thought. *He gets a lady closer to his own status who desires him to court her and he forgets all about me. Not that I'm jealous.*

Or was she jealous? She could not be sure, but somehow, she felt a little irked seeing Griffin clearly enjoying the attentions of another woman.

The archery tournaments and croquet games ended and the dancing began. Griffin led the girl he had been speaking with to the dance floor, while Lucinda was escorted by a man around Griffin's age with whom she was clearly smitten. A dance Shirley thought was called a quadrille began, with young and old dancing on the platform.

Meanwhile, Shirley had shifted from staying in the tent to walking around and pouring tea for those who needed a fresh cup. While she walked, she listened in on their conversations.

"...my coffers have been running low thanks to the imports. I swear, Robert Peel should have been tried and hanged for repealing the Corn Laws!"

"...I must say, it's a pleasure to be out of the house more now. It gets easier to socialize once the children are old enough and you can leave them with the governess or send them to school..."

"...Victoria fancies him? Well, that's certainly upsetting. I cannot compete against Griffin, even if he did spend most of his money on this party..."

"...Lucinda and William make a lovely pair..."

"Where do you suppose Baronet Hunting is? He wouldn't miss his own niece's party, would he?"

"Probably off on some assignation. He was a man of specific appetites back in the day, and I would wager he still is. Either that, or he's too shamefaced to meet with us. But given his history, can you blame him?"

The people who had been discussing Sir Joseph tittered, reminding Shirley of a bunch of noisy geese. Among them was a large, balding gentleman with a walrus-like mustache, who laughed the loudest and the hardiest. He had been the one to make the comment about assignations and the baronet's history. He reminded Shirley of an overstuffed turkey, unaware that it was being fattened up for Christmas dinner.

She kept her tongue, but inside, her contempt for these well-dressed guests, especially the turkey-sized gentleman, smoldered. What did these preening fools know? They had probably not spoken to Sir Joseph in years, so they had no idea what important work he had been doing in the meantime.

Shirley, on the other hand, did know. She had been working with him for a couple of months now, after all. Right now, Sir Joseph was likely deep in the textbooks and monographs he had used to build the Eden Engine, plumbing the depths of the natural world, every crackle of the pages turning over to reveal new knowledge and history, every note bringing him that much closer to changing the world. Why, right now, the baronet was likely—

"My, what's all this then?"

Shirley jumped and whirled around as Sir Joseph appeared by the refreshments' tent, gazing around at the party with a face that neither approved nor disapproved. If Shirley had to give it a name, it was more akin to detached curiosity.

A whisper ran through the guests as everyone turned to look upon the baronet. Even the musicians had stopped playing, though Shirley guessed that was more out of curiosity to see how things played out. On the dancing platform, Lucinda and Griffin both had expressions like they expected an angry bull to turn its attention to them and charge.

"Uncle Joseph," Lucinda said, her voice quavering a little. "I thought you were busy with your research."

"I stepped out to stretch my legs," he replied. "Now again, what's all this?"

He gestured at the party, as if the whole thing were an indescribable mystery. Griffin left the side of the young woman in the red dress and approached Sir Joseph. "It's a garden party, Uncle. Remember? You said I could throw one for Lucinda if I paid for it out of my own pocket?"

"Did I?" The baronet raised a confused eyebrow. "Was I reading a book when you asked?"

"Er, yes sir. While you were eating the previous night's pheasant."

"Ah, no wonder I do not remember that."

"D-Do you disapprove?" asked Lucinda, still wrapped in the arms of the handsome dark-haired young man and looking on the verge of tears.

"Disapprove?" he repeated incredulously. "Why, whatever for? No, go fritter away with your friends and suitors. I do not mind. Though I do wonder, when did it become acceptable to attend any party when one was still dressed in mourning clothes? Oh, never mind. I see some familiar faces are in attendance." He stepped onto the dance platform, a dark gleam in his eyes. "Mrs. Campton, is that you? You're looking well."

Sir Joseph approached a middle-aged woman dancing with a younger man, perhaps her son or nephew. The woman, Mrs. Campton, looked like she had swallowed a lemon. "Um, good to see you as well, Sir Joseph. Have you been well?"

"Very well, thank you," he replied, a dangerous edge to his voice. His eyes alighted on the youth dancing with Mrs. Campton and asked, "Are you a relation of hers, or a servant? If you're the latter, I would be careful. The last servant she danced with suffered a most untimely death. I believe the police are still looking for the knife that did the deed."

The guests gasped. Mrs. Campton, her face that of someone who has received an unexpected punch to the gut, pushed the shocked youth she had been dancing with away as if he were somehow tainted. Unaffected by the atmosphere he had created, Sir Joseph stepped off the platform and approached a handsome man in his mid-thirties and his horse-faced wife.

"Ah, Reginald Douglass! I like the trim of your suit. Made by one of the best tailors in London, no doubt. The only one of its kind too,

I would guess. Goodness, how did you pay for it? The last I heard you were struggling to pay your servants. Too much time at the horse races, is that correct?"

"That's all in the past, Sir Joseph!" said Reginald Douglass, incensed. "I have paid my debts and given up gambling."

"I'm sure you have. But have you found another excuse to get away from the wife you positively loathe?"

Reginald Douglass's horse-faced wife burst into tears and buried her face in her hands. While her husband tried in vain to comfort her and threw insults Sir Joseph's way, Sir Joseph moved onto the gaggle of guests who had laughed like geese when Shirley was refreshing their tea.

"Uncle Joseph, please!" Lucinda cried, tears welling in her eyes. "I thought you said you didn't disapprove!"

But he did not disapprove of the party. That was the thing, Shirley realized. He was fine with the party, so long as he was uninterrupted in his research. It was some of the guests at the party that he objected to. And he was making his objections clear.

"Lord Wyndemere! I haven't seen you in—oh, how long has it been? Well, not since Wilhelmina was still alive, at any rate."

The large gentleman whom Shirley had likened to a large turkey was sweating profusely. He cleared his throat. "Sir Joseph, it's good to see you. Yes, I believe the last time we met, your wife was still alive. It was such a shame, what happened to her. I was deeply sorry to hear about it. She was a wonderful woman."

"Oh, I'm sure you thought so," Sir Joseph replied, the edge in his voice thickening into a deep, throat-spanning anger. "That she was wonderful, that is. You used to visit her quite often, as I recall. I believe you even spent time in her private rooms?"

The entire party inhaled. Sir Joseph sidled up to Lord Wyndemere and bent down to whisper something in his ear. The oversized gentleman's eyes widened to the size of dinner plates and he shot up from his seat.

"Why, I never!" he raged. "You go too far, Sir Joseph! I feel so sorry for your niece's children! They deserve better in a guardian than the likes of you!"

And with that, he stomped off. Sir Joseph watched him go, a sly, satisfied sneer on his face. "Always a pleasure, James. Always a pleasure."

Sir Joseph turned as if to go, and then his eyes alighted on Shirley. "Shirley, what are you doing here?"

For a moment, she did not know how to respond. "Er, I'm helping out, sir," she replied, gesturing with the teapot she held and praying to God it wasn't her turn to receive a verbal lashing. "As a favor to a friend."

Sir Joseph made a disdainful noise in the back of his throat. "Well, I hope your friend is grateful to you. As you well know, your talent is wasted in domestic service." To the curious guests, he revealed, "Shirley Dobbins is my assistant. She'll be a talented scientist someday, given enough training. And if her friends don't prevail upon her good nature too often, of course."

All eyes turned to her, appraising her, no doubt making assumptions about her, her eye, and her relationship to the baronet. Glad that she wasn't on the other end of Sir Joseph's wrath, she merely curtsied and said aloud, "Why thank you, Sir Joseph. You are too kind."

Not how I wanted to be introduced to the wider world as a lab assistant. Especially not at the expense of Lucinda's party. Shirley wondered if Lucinda would forgive her for this and was surprised by how much she cared.

Having finished introducing her, Sir Joseph turned and headed back up to the Lodge, barely glancing at his niece and nephew, or anyone else, as he passed.

***

Despite the fact that the party was supposed to go for another couple of hours, it was clear to Shirley that Sir Joseph's outburst had ended things early. Indeed, it seemed to Shirley that the guests were eager to get out of there. Despite that, Griffin and Lucinda thanked each of the guests personally, even as the latter was unable to keep the tears out of her eyes.

While they were doing that, Shirley helped to clean the party, noticing as she did that there were dark clouds off in the distance. By the time everything had been cleared away, the sun had disappeared behind the clouds and there was a heavy downpour outside. The villagers and the Lodge staff, including Shirley, only just managed to get inside before the deluge fell.

Later, walking aimlessly through the Lodge, Shirley heard sobbing coming from one of the parlor rooms. She glanced through the open door, and spotted Lucinda sitting on a divan and crying into a handkerchief. Nellie sat beside her, stroking her back and whispering encouragement to the older girl that most likely did little to assuage her torment.

Shirley stepped back, intending to move away from the scene, when Lucinda peered up and spotted her. Again, Shirley wondered again if she would be the target of the girl's anger over what had happened at the party. Instead, Lucinda stood up and rushed to her, throwing her arms around Shirley and sobbing into her shoulder. Just like on the day Mr. and Mrs. Avondale had died, Shirley wrapped her arms around the poor girl, unsure what else to do.

"They aren't my real friends."

"What?" Shirley asked.

"They aren't my real friends!" Lucinda repeated vehemently. "The girls who came to the party today! They said they would write and visit again, but I know they won't! After what Uncle Joseph did today, they will want nothing to do with me. I am tainted to them! *Tainted*!"

"Oh, I'm sure that's not true," Shirley replied, though she was not convinced herself. Society friends could be fickle, if what she heard was true. She led Lucinda back to the divan and began stroking her hair. "I'm sure you'll hear from them soon enough."

"You two are my only true friends," Lucinda said, ignoring Shirley's remark and glancing at her and Nellie. "You don't care who my family is or how much money we have. Uncle Joseph pays you, and I know he wouldn't care a fig if either of you were mean to me because I'm no longer your employer. But you two are so nice to me!"

She wailed loudly before devolving into hiccups and sniffles. "Promise me you'll stay my friends. Please?"

"Of course," Shirley assured her.

And she meant it. Somehow, despite the lines that separated their worlds and her behavior when her parents had been alive, Lucinda and Shirley had become friends. And she was fine with that. It was hard to believe that it took a ruined party for Shirley to realize it, but apparently that was how it was.

Hugging her for real this time, she added, "We'll always be friends. You mark my words."

"Yes," Nellie chimed in, hugging Lucinda as well. "We'll always be friends. And we won't ever abandon you."

From the shaking form against her shoulder, Shirley heard a tiny voice say, "Thank you," before disappearing back into sniffles and sobs.

They stayed like that for some time, the only sounds that of Lucinda's weeping and the sky weeping alongside her.

Chapter Ten

Sir Joseph was irritable this afternoon.

Granted, he had been in a black mood since the party on Saturday and had snapped at everyone in the household at least once. Shirley had been snapped at about five times since Monday, and today was Wednesday. But now, with the first test of the Eden Engine on a live subject to occur this afternoon, Sir Joseph was almost wrathful.

As a result, Shirley had made sure to put at least two meters' distance between her and the baronet as he checked and double-checked the consoles, ran over the numbers and his notes multiple times, and consulted his books even more than he consulted his notes. The whole time he muttered to himself, although what he was muttering, Shirley could not say and was unsure she wanted to know.

At the present, Sir Joseph was at his desk reading his books again, rifling through and reading a passage for a minute or so before tossing it aside and picking up another one. Shirley stood outside the ballroom, hoping to avoid being the target of the baronet's wrath for the third time that day. That, and she was waiting for Milverton to deliver an essential component to their experiment. Without it, they would be unable to turn on the Eden Engine.

Shirley hoped that once the component arrived, the experiment would be a success. Otherwise, Sir Joseph's temper was sure to resemble a volcano, like the one in the Natural Sciences book she had read last night, Mount Vesuvius, which had covered an entire city in lava when it erupted.

As if in answer to her prayers, Milverton appeared beside her, holding a paperboard box in his hands. From the box came a snuffling noise that Shirley recognized immediately.

"One piglet with a missing leg," he intoned dully when he reached her. "Delivered only a few minutes ago."

Shirley took the box from him, surprised by how light it was. She peaked inside. Sure enough, there was a piglet with three legs inside. It was a bit smaller than the average piglet of its age and was busily munching on a bowl full of mush.

"Thank you, Mr. Milverton," she said. "We're really lucky to have this one. Sir Joseph is extremely grateful, and so am I. I hope you let Mr. Amberley know that."

Mr. Amberley was the farmer whose sow had given birth to the three-legged piglet. He had been of the opinion that a piglet with only three legs would be of less worth than the runt of the litter and wanted to kill it, but his young daughter had taken a liking to it and decided to raise it herself. When Sir Joseph had sent word to the villages that he was looking for animals with defects or wounds that had proven stubborn in healing, Mr. Amberley had been the first to answer the call. In exchange for a couple of shillings, of course.

"I will, Ms. Dobbins," Milverton replied. A grimace passed over his face as he said her name. It appeared he still was not fond of addressing her as an equal. "Especially after he related to me that his daughter, little Molly, was quite upset at losing the piglet."

Shirley glanced down at the piglet and noticed a distinctive spot along its side. It reminded her of a four-pointed star, oddly enough. She had a feeling that little Molly Amberley had memorized that star-shaped spot and considered it a sign that this piglet was her piglet, was no one else's, and was quite special.

She looked back up at Milverton and replied, "Well, if all goes well, she'll be getting her pig back, and better than ever." And without waiting for a response, she turned and slipped into the laboratory.

"What is it?"

She jumped, jostling the piglet in its box. It squealed in protest, but Shirley barely heard it over the blood pounding in her ears. She had been so excited to bring the piglet in and present it to Sir Joseph, she had forgotten he was in a less-than-cheerful state of mind.

"Um, the piglet sir," she said, managing to keep the tremor from her voice. "It's here."

Sir Joseph looked up from his book. Immediately his furrowed brows smoothed and an apologetic expression replaced his previous anger.

"Oh Shirley," he said. "Forgive me for my outburst just now. Bring the test subject here. Set it anywhere, I don't care."

Shirley brought the piglet over and set its box on a pile of books. Some of the titles she recognized and had read herself as part of her training as a lab assistant: Charles Darwin's *On the Origins of the Species*; Peter Ewart's *On the measure of moving force*; *The Scientific Papers of James Prescott Joule*, published by the London Physical Society; and of course, the collected works of Plato.

Others, however, were too advanced for her at her current level. Which was a shame, because they were the texts that Sir Joseph had relied on the most in his creation of the Eden Engine. Ptolemy of Alexandria's *Apocrypha*; Davros's *Treatise on Dimensional Architecture and Engineering*; and R. Gold's *Directory of the Realms*. Shirley had wanted to read them almost as soon as she began to grasp scientific concepts, but Sir Joseph said she was not ready for the secrets hidden within them. She supposed it would be several years yet before she could even touch the books, if that was the case.

Sir Joseph coughed, pulling Shirley from her thoughts on the books. "Shirley," he said.

"Yes sir?"

He was silent for a moment, then said, "I know that I have...been rather difficult to get along with as of late. Especially towards you. I-I would like to apologize for my behavior. You do not deserve any of it and I am a disgrace of a man for taking my anger out on you."

Shirley was taken aback. She was not used to her employers apologizing to her, especially when they were not young society ladies desperate for friendship and affection. "D-Don't think anything of it, sir," she said after a moment's hesitation. "We all have our bad days."

"Yes, well...my bad days were caused by seeing that man at that party," he admitted. "Lord Wyndemere."

Shirley paused. What was the appropriate response in this situation? "I-I see," she said finally.

"I'm afraid you do not," Sir Joseph replied, not unkindly, with a heavy sigh. "I'm sure you are aware of my past scandals. If you did not know them before you came here, then someone has likely told you by now." When Shirley nodded stiffly, he continued, "Lord Wyndemere was one of my wife's paramours, of that I'm sure. I spotted him leaving the Lodge in a carriage one afternoon as I was returning from a hunting trip. He was in a hurry, as if he did not want anyone to know he had been there. And when I found my wife, she was taking an afternoon bath. She said she 'was in the mood to wash herself while it was still light out.' But I know. She was trying to erase the scent of her lover from her."

"I-I'm sorry," Shirley stammered. Then, before she could stop herself or think of the ramifications, asked, "Was that what you whispered to him at the party? That you knew he was her lover?"

Sir Joseph shook his head. "I told him that my son was, in truth, *his* son."

Shirley inhaled. She wanted him to stop talking. She wanted to tell Sir Joseph that this conversation was going beyond the boundaries of master and employee. But it seemed the baronet was determined to tell her everything, because before she could open her mouth, he elaborated, "I cannot be certain, you understand. Paternity is not something easily proven when the child resembles neither mother nor father. However, I do know that at the time Wesley was conceived, both Lord Wyndemere and I had relations with my wife. Not at the same time, obviously. But within the same month, which is reason enough to be suspicious. And even if he was not Wesley's father, he certainly had an effect on the boy."

"What do you mean?" Shirley heard herself say.

"Lord Wyndemere continued to visit my wife during the pregnancy," Sir Joseph explained. "Anytime I was away on business or out hunting, he was there, ready to resume relations with a pregnant woman. As I am sure you're aware, a gestating baby is influenced by the men and women the mother comes into contact with during the pregnancy. All this has been scientifically proven." His voice took a dangerous edge again as he said, "Lord Wyndemere is a large, stupid man with a large head but little brain. And Wesley, my son, was large and stupid, with an enlarged head caused by the accumulation of water within his skull, which subsequently shrunk his brain. I am certain that this condition eventually contributed to my son's early demise.

"So, one way or another, I blame my son's condition, and his death, on that pompous fool. And to find him on my estate again after all these years—well, you can see why I have been in such a state."

"I'm so sorry," Shirley said after a pause. An idea came to her, and she added, "But once we perfect the Eden Engine, no one will suffer like your son again. Why, perhaps in a hundred years, you'll be praised as the man who helped solve many of mankind's problems!"

A small smile poked out from between the baronet's lips. "Thank you, Shirley. You know exactly what to say." Then he surprised her by gently cupping her cheek in his hand and adding, "My dear."

Shirley froze, shocked. At first, she thought Sir Joseph was trying to seduce her. But that did not seem to be the case. The look in Sir Joseph's eyes was different. There was tenderness there, but not the sort of tenderness one showed to someone they wanted to be their lover. No, this was a form of compassion Shirley did not recognize. What did it mean? And was it appropriate for Sir Joseph to show it to her?

Before she could consider the matter any further, Sir Joseph dropped his hand and said, "Well, enough dwelling on the past. Let's get to work and proceed with the experiment."

He picked up the paperboard box and carried the piglet to the Engine, all traces of his earlier rage gone. Shirley stared after him for a couple of seconds before dashing to join him. Sir Joseph set the box down in front of Console Seven and slid back the bombardment chamber door. He then lifted the piglet out of the box and set it on the platform before sliding the door back into place and locking it. The piglet stood unsteadily on its three legs, sniffing and snorting as it took in its new surroundings.

Meanwhile, Shirley took her place at Console One, gripping the handle of a switch. Sir Joseph gave the command and she pulled the switch down. Then she ran across the room and pulled an identical switch on Console Thirteen. At once, both consoles began to hum as they sent electric power down the wires to the other consoles.

In the bombardment chamber, the piglet snorted nervously.

"Shirley, Console Four!" Sir Joseph commanded.

Even before the command was out, however, Shirley was already there, turning dials and measuring readouts from the gauges. Atop the console, two gyroscopes began to spin at high speeds within a glass dome. She then ran to Console Twelve and pressed several buttons. Levers turned and pulled within the machine casing, making a loud clunking noise.

On the other side of the Engine, Sir Joseph was switching between Consoles Five and Six, activating different functions at prearranged moments, setting various mechanisms into motion. He ran past Shirley on his way to Console Nine, who was monitoring things on Console Eight. The whole time, a smell like ozone was filling the laboratory while electricity crackled above and between the consoles. Within the vacuum tubes, a strange light floated through them towards Console Seven.

The energy of the Pure World had been summoned.

As the clanging, humming, buzzing, and whirring from the Engine reached its climax, Sir Joseph and Shirley met at Console Seven. Within the bombardment chamber, the piglet had pissed and shat itself in fear and was desperately banging its body against the glass in an effort to free itself. They ignored it as they grabbed the handle of the final switch, the one that would release the pure energy into the chamber. Sir Joseph locked eyes with Shirley and nodded.

They pulled the switch.

The gargantuan console roared, its lights blinking on and off as streams of the pure energy flowed through the tubes and into the bombardment chamber like pressurized water from multiple fire hoses. The piglet gave a terrified squeal as it disappeared within the light.

The next ten seconds felt like an eternity. Finally, Sir Joseph and Shirley threw the switch back into the off position and ran around the Engine, shutting everything down. As they did, the noise died, and the light of the pure energy dissipated, leaving only a gray dust on the glass of the vacuum tubes and the bombardment chamber. When the Engine had fully shut down and the laboratory was once again only lit by low electric lighting, they rushed to Console Seven and stared through the glass.

At the bottom of the bombardment chamber was the piglet, still alive and with a fourth leg growing where one had been missing previously.

The experiment was a success!

Shirley and Sir Joseph locked eyes again. She could not contain herself. She screamed and jumped for joy. "A success! A success! The experiment's a success!"

Oh, Molly Amberley is going to be surprised when she finds her pig is no longer a burden on the farm!

Sir Joseph smiled indulgently as he unlocked the chamber and slid the glass door back. He picked up the piglet and held it up as the leg finished growing into place. It was a perfect little leg, covered in tiny, bristly hairs and ending in a split hoof. The baronet's grin was so wide, it threatened to meet his earlobes.

"Welcome to the new age, little creature," he whispered. The piglet gave a tired snort in response.

With a soft chuckle, he handed the animal to Shirley, who gladly took it in her arms and began stroking its back. "Congratulations," she whispered to it. "You're the first of many happy endings."

There was a loud *POP!* and Shirley's vision became a curtain of red as something wet and warm flew into her eyes. At the same time, the pig in her arms became lighter and quieter. Somewhere in front of her, Sir Joseph whispered, "Oh my goodness."

Shirley wiped whatever had landed in her eyes away with a sleeve, but all that did was put more detritus in her eyes. Sir Joseph told her wait. A second later he was patting her face with his silk handkerchief, clearing away the grime. When she could see again, Shirley glanced down to see what had happened. She found herself covered in gore and viscera all along the front of her dress. And in her arms, the piglet was nothing more than a mess of skin over a bone frame, its back gaping open like a giant mouth.

In an instant, she grasped what had happened and dropped the piglet's carcass. It made a wet splat as it hit the ground, blood leaking out of its back and onto the parquet floor. She backed away, suddenly cold despite the warm blood all over her face.

"Shirley," said Sir Joseph.

"It-it failed," she said, blood dripping into her mouth. The smell of death clogged her nose, and the decision to never eat pork again flitted through her mind as she grappled with what had occurred. "The experiment failed. The piglet's dead. Oh God, it's dead. What will we tell little Molly Amberley? Her piglet's dead. Oh God. What now? The experiment failed, it's failed, it—!"

Sir Joseph jumped over the carcass, grabbed her by the shoulders, and pulled her into a hug before she could grow more hysterical. The gesture surprised Shirley into silence. She had not expected it. A good shoulder shake was often the first resort for a woman on the verge of a breakdown.

Nonetheless, it did the trick, and Shirley felt her mind calm. She was still in shock and horrified by what had happened, but at least she was no longer on the verge of going mad.

When he let her go, Shirley was appalled to see that the entire front of Sir Joseph's shirt and lab coat, as well as his expensive silk cravat, were stained with blood. Before she could open her mouth to express her dismay, however, he dismissed it with a wave of his hand.

"Don't worry about it, my dear," he said, using that strange term of endearment again. "Anyway, you go upstairs and get cleaned up."

"W-What about the mess?" she asked, gesturing at the carcass and the blood and entrails scattered everywhere. "And what about you?"

Again, he dismissed it with a wave of his hand. "I'll have Mrs. Preston and the other maids come in and help me clean it up. Then I will go and take a bath. For now though, you just go upstairs and wash that mess off your face. That's an order."

She opened her mouth to protest, but blood fell on her teeth and tongue as she did. Close to retching, she shut her mouth, nodded in thanks, and turned to leave. She took measured footsteps all the way to the door. However, the moment she was clear of the ballroom, she ran.

Chapter Eleven

Shirley stumbled dazedly down the hallway towards the washroom, her mind still filled with visions of the failed experiment downstairs. It kept playing over and over in her mind, like a gramophone whose needle keeps sticking on a scratch in the record. She felt the hope, joy and triumph as the piglet's leg grew into place, only to be crushed by the horror and disappointment as it exploded in her arms, over and over again.

Where do we go from here? she wondered. *It took Sir Joseph years just to get to this point. How long will it take to get the Engine ready before we can experiment with a live subject again? Will we ever try again, now that we know what could happen should we fail?*

The thought of not trying again scared her nearly as much as the thought of trying again. Although she had started out as a reluctant assistant to the baronet, she was now as invested in the Engine's success as he was. The Engine was the hope of humanity, the key to curing its physical imperfections and its mental evils. Without it...

Without the Engine, more little girls will be born with eyes like mine. Without it, more women will drink themselves to death, like my mother. Without it, more men will become madmen and murderers looking for the women who poisoned them. Just like—

"Shirley! Where are you going?"

Shirley stopped and turned around to see Lucinda hurrying towards her. The younger girl came to a hard stop as she took in Shirley's blood-spattered dress and face, a hand reaching up to her mouth as it formed an "o" of horror.

"My Lord," she whispered. "Shirley, what happened? You look like death!"

"The experiment failed," Shirley replied quietly, her tone numb. She could not even muster the energy to react to Lucinda's show of sympathy, whether it be with annoyance like before or with gratitude now that they were friends.

Lucinda stood still and thought for a moment before reaching out, twirling Shirley around by the relatively unstained parts of her sleeves and directing her down the hall at breakneck speed. "Come on, let's get you into a bath," she said. "Before someone sees you and thinks you're one of the Ripper's victims."

Shirley shivered at the comment, but Lucinda did not seem to notice.

A couple minutes later, Shirley was sitting in a chair in the washroom while Lucinda turned on the water heater attached to the porcelain, claw-footed tub. The brass device roared to life, chugging and sputtering before proceeding to spew steaming water into the tub. She made a few adjustments with the faucets, then nodded with satisfaction before going to help Shirley out of her dress.

It was then that Shirley began to feel like herself again and glanced behind her. "You don't have to undress me," she said as Lucinda began undoing the buttons on the back of her dress. "I'm not a child. I dress myself fine every morning."

"This is not every morning," Lucinda replied. "This is after whatever you do with Uncle Joseph went horribly wrong. Now let me do this for you. You do enough for me all the time."

That silenced Shirley and she let Lucinda help her out of her dress, petticoat, corset, stockings, chemise and undergarments. With the last of her clothes on the floor, Shirley went to the sink to wash the blood and grime off her body before slipping into the bath. She sighed; after the horror in the laboratory, it felt like heaven.

"Is the water too hot?" Lucinda asked.

Shirley shook her head. "No, it's perfect. Thank you."

Lucinda smiled. "You're welcome. Now, if you'll excuse me, I'll find you something clean to wear."

She gathered up Shirley's clothes, making sure to bury her bloodstained dress in the center of the ball of petticoats and stockings, and exited the washroom. Alone, Shirley lowered herself up to her lips in the water, enjoying the heat as it seeped to the very core of her being.

She sat there a few minutes, just allowing herself to indulge and delight in the bath without thought or notion, before sitting up again and pulling a bar of soap off a tiny shelf set into the wall. As she was soaping herself, Lucinda returned with a fresh set of clothes.

"Feeling better?" she asked.

"Much better," Shirley replied. "God, I love these baths."

Lucinda laughed as she placed the clothes on a cabinet table and sat down in the chair Shirley had been in not ten minutes before. "I agree, they really are delightful. Though I wonder if enjoying them too much might be bad for you. Perhaps they lead to fits or immorality."

Shirley gave her a raised eyebrow. "What are you on about?"

Lucinda laughed. "Just something in a book my mother read once. Apparently bathing can cause insanity and immoral behavior if the water is too hot. And bathing in water that is too cold can cause hives, indigestion and fatigue in women. As well as insanity."

The two girls stared at each other for a moment. Then they burst into laughter. "Who comes up with that stuff?" Shirley asked. "I've taken baths at least once a week since I turned twelve, and no matter the temperature, I never saw any of that."

"You did?" Lucinda asked, confused. "I never knew. Did you bathe at my parents' house?"

"I went to the public baths in London," Shirley answered with a shake of her head. "I went in, cleaned myself up, and got a bit of time to myself too. It was quite relaxing. And even better, it only cost a penny."

"Oh really?" Lucinda replied, keenly interested now. "I never went to them. Mother always said they were low-class and unhygienic."

"Well, they kind of are," Shirley mused. "Low class, I mean." She ducked her head under the water, held it for a moment, and then rose.

Spitting water out of her mouth, she continued, "But I can see why your mother would say it was unhygienic. If you used the bathing pool, you had to bathe with twenty to forty people at a time, and half of them would be children playing in the water. The only thing keeping those who just wanted a quiet bath from them was a simple rope stretched across the pool. If you paid a couple more pennies, however, you got your own stall. A never-ending stream of water falling on your head and all the privacy you could want. I usually bought a private stall for special occasions, like Christmas or my birthday."

"Wait, I think I've heard of those stalls!" said Lucinda, excited. "The French call them douche baths, I think. They're supposed to not only be really fancy, but good for you as well. I wonder why Uncle Joseph hasn't installed them in any of the washrooms here yet."

Shirley shrugged. Standing up, she wrapped a robe around herself and stepped out of the bath, sighing happily.

"I needed that," she said. "Thanks for helping me, Lucinda. I feel like myself again—Lucinda?"

As Shirley was speaking, Lucinda jumped out of the chair and backed into a corner, staring across the washroom with a terror-stricken face. Eyebrow raised, Shirley followed her gaze and saw something small, dark grey bordering on black, and furry. A rat. It stood on its hind legs, fur standing on end and making a throaty, honking growl. It was a clear warning that the beast was enraged and would attack if provoked.

At once, Shirley's instincts from growing up in dosshouses and on the streets, where the rats sometimes became big enough to hunt cats, kicked into life. In two quick bounds, she grabbed the chair Lucinda had been sitting in and, holding it up in front of her like a shield, backed into the corner with Lucinda.

"Stay behind me and don't move a muscle!" she commanded.

All she received was a sniffle in response. She glanced behind her. Lucinda was crying. "I-I hate rats," she said. "When I was three, there was one in the closet. It-it—!"

"I understand," Shirley interrupted. She had had her own bad encounters with rats before and had learned long ago how to deal with them. The first thing to do, of course, was to get over your fear of the little brutes, and she had done that long ago. "But I'll get us out of here. It's more afraid of us than we are of it. So if we give it a route of escape and aren't between it and anything it wants, it should—what the bloody fuck?"

In the two seconds Shirley had taken her eyes off the rodent, it had been joined by allies. Several allies. At least forty more. They stood in three long rows, hissing and baring their fangs at the two girls.

A bead of sweat ran down Shirley's temple. Behind her, Lucinda whimpered helplessly. "W-What are we going to do?" she asked in a tiny voice.

Shirley tried to think. Screaming felt natural, but there was a chance that might set the rats off. The same problem arose with making any other noise. They could climb out the window behind them, but they were on the second floor. Could they survive a fall from that height? And Shirley was wearing a bathrobe and nothing else. If she were to end up in a compromising situation by climbing out the window—

One of the rats flung itself at them before she could finish working through her options. Lucinda let loose a high-pitched scream, while Shirley swung the chair, one of the legs slamming into the rat and sending it ricocheting into the tub with a pitiful squeak and a splash. As if waiting for this, the rest of the rats rushed forward, many of them leaping across the washroom towards them.

Lucinda screamed again, clutching Shirley's shoulders so tightly they hurt. Shirley, meanwhile, stepped forward with the chair upraised. The only way out would be to rush through the little bastards while pushing them back with the chair, hope they did not sustain too many bites, and get out as quickly as possible.

"Shirley!" Lucinda cried.

"Don't let go of me, whatever you do!" she shouted, quieting her own fear. Now was not the time to hesitate. Hesitation meant bites, which meant disease and probable death.

Three rats leapt at them, their mouths wide open to reveal large, yellow teeth. With a defiant scream, Shirley rushed forward and swung the chair. It connected with two of the furry little missiles, while the third glanced off it and bounced off the wall. Lucinda screamed as the rat fell dazed beside her but kept following behind Shirley as they continued forward. Several rats tried to attack from the ground in a wide semicircle, while Shirley swept the chair legs across the floor in front of her. The rats stopped and drew back a little, as if reassessing their plan of attack.

Come on, you little beasts, she thought, grinning somehow despite the situation. *I may have never fought an army of you, but I know how to keep you all back. Just bloody try me.*

She waited for the rats to make a move, but all they did was hiss and bare their teeth. Shirley bared hers as well. "Come on then!" she shouted. "What are you so afraid of?"

The rats leapt at them all at once, one of them landing on the sleeve of her robe. It squeaked, nearly fell off, and then found its balance before readjusting its fat, hairy body for another leap. Shirley suddenly regretted egging the little beasts on.

"Leave her alone!" Lucinda's hand swept across Shirley's arm from behind her shoulder, knocking the rat off and sending it flying into the wall. The moment the rat hit the wall, the lights flickered on and off with an electric buzz before plunging the washroom into darkness.

For the longest second in the history of time, all was silent. Shirley waited for the rending of flesh and the sound of screams as the other rats attacked, but nothing happened. The washroom was totally silent, save for the sound of their breathing.

And then the lights flickered on again. The rats were gone.

Shirley and Lucinda stared in astonishment. "Where did they go?" the latter asked in a trembling voice.

"I-I don't know," Shirley replied, eyes roving around the washroom. Not only were the rats gone, there were no signs they had ever been here. No scuffs or scratch marks on the tile, no lost patches of fur or droppings. Even the bathwater was clear of large, furry bodies. If someone had walked in at that moment, they would have seen nothing odd, save for the two girls huddled in the corner, one of them brandishing a chair like a weapon, and—

Dust. There was a black dust all over the tiled floor. Shirley had not noticed it before, as she had been focused on the rats, but now that she saw it, she could not unsee it. And now that she thought about it, where had she seen that dust before?

The washroom door crashed open, and Mrs. Preston and Griffin stumbled in, both shouting for an explanation for the screaming. Their sudden appearance frightened Shirley and Lucinda into screaming again, while Griffin cried out and turned towards the door as he saw that Shirley was wearing only a flimsy bathrobe. Meanwhile Mrs. Preston, seeing neither girl was in mortal danger, repeated her question of what had happened.

"Rats!" Lucinda shouted. "There were rats in here! An army of them!"

"An army of them?" Griffin repeated, still looking out at the hallway.

Shirley opened her mouth to correct Lucinda, but from behind her came a moan. Recognizing the meaning of that moan, Shirley turned around and caught Lucinda as she fainted. With Mrs. Preston's help, she laid Lucinda on the ground while assuring her brother that his younger sister was alright.

"Was there really an army of rats in here?" Mrs. Preston asked as she placed a towel under Lucinda's head and took her pulse.

"More like thirty or forty," Shirley clarified, placing the chair down. "But they acted like an army. Attacked us all at once."

"Were either of you bit?" Griffin asked, his voice vibrating with the struggle to keep control.

Shirley shook her head. "We're fine, thank God. I fought them off and they just...left, I guess. I don't know where they went. Lucinda knocked one off my arm, the lights went off and then they were gone."

"She did?" When Griffin spoke again, he sounded impressed. "How about that. She's normally terrified of the little beasts. That was brave of her."

"Brave or not, the shock has had a bad effect on her," Mrs. Preston advised. "You should take Miss Lucinda and leave this room immediately. Find someplace safe to recover. I'll have Beth bring up tea momentarily. Mr. Avondale, go summon the Master and Mr. Milverton and let them know what happened. We cannot allow rats to have free reign in the Hunting Lodge!"

Griffin's retreating footsteps echoed down the hallway, while Shirley pulled Lucinda up and carried her like an invalid out the washroom and to the latter's bedroom, which was closest. Behind them, Shirley heard Mrs. Preston muttering about how Sir Joseph would have to approve renovations and a larger staff now that two women had been attacked by rats.

Shirley was not sure if Sir Joseph would approve anything beyond rat traps and maybe some poison if nobody had been hurt. However, Shirley had bigger concerns now. First there had been the hands coming out of the toilet bowl. Then there had been Cutbush and the maze in the library. And now an army of rats had appeared and disappeared in the space of a minute.

Griffin was right, something was very wrong at the Hunting Lodge. And if something was not done soon to alleviate the situation, Shirley did not think any of them would live for very much longer.

Chapter Twelve

As Shirley had predicted, the incident with the rats did not compel Sir Joseph to hire a larger staff or to approve renovations to the Hunting Lodge. Instead, he simply hired some men from the Further Village to come over one afternoon and search the place for rats' nests and place down some traps. At the end of the day, all they had found was a single small nest, which they easily caught and herded into a cage. To Shirley's dismay, these rats were not the ones she and Lucinda had seen in the washroom. They were much smaller and showed no aggression whatsoever.

The rat catchers left and Sir Joseph considered the matter of the rats closed, despite Lucinda's insistence that those were not the rats she had seen and that another search needed to be conducted. Shirley stayed silent. She was not sure another search would do any good, if the rats came from the same source as the arms in the toilet bowl and the Cutbush lookalike.

With the issue of the rats supposedly taken care of, life continued unobstructed. July arrived with its normal levels of heat and humidity, and the Hunting Lodge opened its windows and turned on the electrically powered ceiling fans. Out in the villages and on the farms, the residents changed out of their thicker clothes into articles made of hemp or cotton and with fewer layers. Even Lucinda, who was still required to wear mourning garb for a few more months, changed from her heavy crepe dresses to hemp ones dyed black, and did not object to having the sleeves shortened and the neckline brought down a little.

The only place within Sir Joseph's domain not to change with the passing of seasons was the laboratory. Within, the thick, black curtains were always drawn, and the Eden Engine always gave off enough heat to make the entire north wing of the Lodge feel like the surface of the sun.

Despite the heat, Sir Joseph and Shirley kept working within the laboratory, day in and day out, up to twelve hours a day sometimes. By the middle of the month, work had progressed enough on the Engine that they felt confident to try with live subjects again.

"The problem last time was that the energy of the Pure World was diluted by our impure world," Sir Joseph had said a week after the incident with the piglet. During the preceding seven days, he had gone over the entirety of the Engine, as well as reviewed all his notes with a fine-toothed comb. "When the pure energy is diluted too much, it's unable to make the necessary corrections to the test subject's imperfections. So, for our next experiment, we have to make sure the energy is as undiluted as possible until the subject's imperfections are corrected."

This had been the direction of the work these past several weeks. And now they were ready.

Or at least, the Engine and Sir Joseph was ready. Shirley, who had thought she was ready, was unsure. Especially now that she was looking at the sleeping kitten that had been delivered earlier today to the Lodge by one of the shopkeepers from the village.

"You seem distracted today, my dear," Sir Joseph remarked, stepping beside her and placing a hand on her shoulder. "Is everything alright?"

Shirley shrugged. In addition to her work and her scientific studies, she had been trying to figure out what could cause such horrifying visions as the arms in the toilet, Cutbush in the library, and the rats in the washroom. She had revisited the exact places where those incidents had occurred several times over the past few weeks, perused every book she could find for an explanation, and had even gone down to the villages to talk to the locals about the history in the area in case that had something to do with it.

All to no avail. And what was even stranger, she had tried and failed multiple times to talk to Griffin Avondale, the only other person she knew who was interested in solving this mystery. Whenever she tried to find him, however, he was always out of the Lodge. Where he went and what he did, she was not sure, but she could not help but feel he was avoiding her.

Perhaps her attempts to put some distance between herself and the besotted young man had worked too well. And she had no idea if she was happy or annoyed by that.

But that was not what was bothering her about today's experiment. "I just don't want a repeat of the piglet," she replied. "Especially not with a kitten."

She reached down into its box and stroked the back of the sleeping creature. It did not wake or even stir at her touch, most likely due to being sedated. Sir Joseph believed that the piglet, who had been awake during the last experiment, had contributed to its own doom by releasing its urine and feces before the pure energy had been released. The solution, according to the baronet, was to make sure the test subject had relieved itself prior to the experiment and then sedate it so it would not be frightened and soil itself like the piglet did.

"Nothing is more emblematic of imperfection or impurity than the need to relieve ourselves of waste products in so disgusting a manner," Sir Joseph had surmised while explaining the improvements they would make to the Engine to prevent further dilution. "Even our noble society, obsessed with all the wrong things in its pursuit for some strange definition of 'respectability,' has the right of this. The whole of the peerage like to pretend none of them need to relieve themselves. Especially the women of society."

It was an exaggeration, of course, if only slight, and Shirley had laughed at the time. However, there had been a serious meaning behind it, and so when the kitten had been brought to them earlier today, they had mixed a drug into its food so it would sleep uninterrupted for a few hours.

"I understand how you feel, my dear," Sir Joseph assured her. By this point, Shirley was used to the term of endearment and did not mind it so much. Instead, she took it as a sign that Sir Joseph trusted her and valued her assistance. "But think of the alternative. That kitten was born blind and deaf. It can only get around through smell and feel, and even then, it is prone to life-threatening accidents. Mr. Hartley in the village wanted to kill it the moment he found out. After all, a deaf or blind cat makes for a terrible mouser. One that is deaf *and* blind has no chance at all!"

"And only the promise of a few coins has kept it alive," Shirley finished. "I know. This is the only chance that kitten has of living a productive life."

"Then I suggest we get started," he said. "Before much more time gets on and that little creature wakes up."

Shirley nodded and, steeling herself for what was to come, laid the kitten in its box outside the bombardment chamber. From there, she and Sir Joseph switched on the Engine, and then began the process of gathering up the pure energy again. The major difference this time, however, was that they withheld placing the kitten in the bombardment chamber until the chamber had been sanitized with a short blast of pure energy, right at the moment when the Engine was at its loudest.

As Shirley placed the kitten in the bombardment chamber and locked it in, she said a little prayer for it to come through the experiment in perfect health. Then, grabbing the final switch with Sir Joseph, they released the pure energy into the bombardment chamber.

Bright light poured in and the Engine roared. Shirley and Sir Joseph waited ten seconds as the pure energy swirled around the chamber before pushing the switch back into the off position and running around the laboratory to turn the engine off. With the Engine switched off, they returned to Console Seven and peered in through the smudged and dirty glass of the bombardment chamber.

The kitten stood in the center of the chamber, awake and on all fours. Whether it had woken up because of the noise of the Engine or because of the effects of the pure energy, neither Shirley nor Sir Joseph could say. However, awake it was, and it was mewling as if it were in pain.

For a moment, Shirley was certain something had gone wrong again and the kitten would end up just like the piglet. When it did not explode or otherwise exhibit signs that the experiment had ended in failure, Shirley wondered why it sounded the way it did.

Then she noticed how it would open its eyes briefly before quickly shutting them again, and the truth washed over her.

"It's sensitive to the light," she said to Sir Joseph. "It's not used to being able to see. Quick, we have to get it out of the chamber!"

Sir Joseph nodded and undid the lock on the chamber. Even before he had pushed it all the way back, Shirley had reached in and scooped the kitten into her arms. With a soft mewl, it buried its head in the crook of her elbow. She whispered soft shushing noises and gently petted its back. In response, the kitten began to purr and even poked its head out to get a quick peek at her before hiding its face again in her elbow.

With a sigh of relief, Shirley smiled at Sir Joseph. "I think it will be alright," she whispered. "It wasn't used to all the noise and light. Must have been painful for it."

Realization dawned on Sir Joseph's face, and he spoke in a whisper to match hers. "Yes, my dear, I think you're right. That's something we had not considered, how the test subjects will react once their imperfections have been relieved. But I daresay, after some time, it should become used to its new senses. Well done on you for realizing that, Shirley."

Shirley blushed. "Thank you, Sir Joseph. I'm glad to be of assistance—hang on. What's all that?"

Shirley pointed to the glass door of the bombardment chamber. It was covered in a coating of black dust, dust that she had seen before in the aftermath of the first experiment, and after the vacuum tubes had broken apart. As well as after the incident with the arms in the toilet, after the appearance of Cutbush in the library, and after the rat attack in the washroom.

"You mean I never explained to you what that dust is?" Sir Joseph asked, his voice rising a little in tone. He held up his finger for her to wait, then retreated to the back of the laboratory. A moment later, he returned with a tiny brush and a glass slide for a microscope. Stepping carefully into the bombardment chamber, he brushed a little of the ash onto the slide before placing a segment of clear adhesive tape over the dust. He then gestured for her to follow him to one of the workbenches, where a microscope sat under a leather cover.

Sir Joseph pulled the cover off, switched an electric bulb underneath the platform on and slid the glass slide onto the platform. He then stepped aside and gestured for her to look through the microscope's eyepiece. Shirley leaned forward, glanced through the eyepiece, and stared a moment before turning back to Sir Joseph.

In her scientific studies, Sir Joseph had shown her several different specimen samples underneath the microscope. She had seen the square and rectangular cells of cork trees and rose stems, the spores that caused anthrax disease, the round cells that lined the sides of her mouth, and even tiny microbes with long, elephant-like arms used to capture prey that existed in most waters. The microscope could illuminate everything that could not be seen with the naked eye.

At least, that had been what Shirley had thought. But as she had glanced down the eyepiece, she had seen nothing in the slide. No microbes, no particles, no cells, nothing. Just a blank, white space. And yet when she checked the slide, the black dust was there, darkening the glass as sure as she stood there.

"How is that possible?" she asked.

Sir Joseph grinned as if he had been hoping for this reaction. "That, my dear, is known as holy ash," he explained. "Known as *vibhuti* in Hindu. It often appears during sacred rituals to the Hindu gods, and is considered a sign of pure divine power having been accessed and harnessed during the rituals. That ash produces no smell or taste, and you cannot feel it on your fingers if you touch it. And, as you can see, it does not appear under the microscope. And yet, it is there. A mystery that may never be understood, though we strive to."

"It's a sign of divine power being accessed and harnessed?" Shirley repeated in amazement.

The baronet nodded. "And it appears when pure energy is siphoned from the Pure World. After all, what is the Pure World if not divine? The perfect forms of all things and beings exist there. In fact, I believe the Garden of Eden was a manifestation of the Pure World in our imperfect world, and that Adam and Eve were perfect beings in that world. It was only when man ate of the Forbidden Fruit—likely a fruit native to this world rather than the Pure World—that humanity became imperfect."

"So, human beings were originally from the Pure World?" Shirley asked. "And when we were 'sinless,' that just meant we were pure and hadn't been tainted by anything impure from this world?"

"Well, that's my hypothesis," Sir Joseph replied. "I cannot be certain unless I find the Garden of Eden, can I? But enough about that. Now that we have discovered a way for animals to survive the process, we will need to prepare for our first human trials. I will study my texts, and Shirley...I want you to monitor the kitten."

"Sir?" Shirley asked, confused.

"I want you to monitor the kitten," he repeated. "Feed it, care for it, and see how it develops. If there are any ill side effects or it returns to an enfeebled state, that will be important to know for further testing."

Even as he was saying it though, Shirley realized there was a double meaning behind the baronet's words. Sir Joseph was not only giving her a command to monitor the kitten's condition going forward: he was giving it to her as a present. The kitten was to be her pet.

"A-Are you sure?" she asked.

Sir Joseph nodded. "I'm certain. And I suggest you give the kitten a name. We cannot keep calling it 'the kitten,' after all."

Oh God, he really wants to give it to me as a pet, she thought. In all her life, she had never wanted a pet. In homes with pets, the owners played and petted their dogs and cats, but left the task of feeding and cleaning up after them to the servants. Lord Above help you if sweet little Sir Orange or the drooling devil Maxwell disliked you for whatever reason. Or worse, preferred your company over that of their master's.

And yet, she could not say no to Sir Joseph. Not after all he had done for her.

Shirley glanced down at the kitten, still curled up in her arms with its head buried in the crook of her elbows. However, now it was curled with its belly towards her, and it was purring softly. It was no longer in pain. She reached over absently with one hand and scratched it on the back. It turned a bit more, the better to take advantage of her hand, and Shirley realized it was female.

Names for a female kitten, she thought. *Josephine? Dinah? Mrs. Norris, perhaps? No, none of those sound right. She has white fur, maybe something like that. Snowball or Snowflake? No, much too obvious. But maybe a word for white in another language. Blanche? Blanca? Bianca? Why so many B's? Strange about that, because the root word in Latin is* album, *and that begins with an A—*

And then it hit her. "Albedo. I'll name her Albedo."

Sir Joseph smiled. "The Latin word for 'whiteness.' I like it. Now I suggest you get Albedo back in her box and take her somewhere you can keep track of her, my dear. I'll apprise you of what our plans are going forward in the morning."

Shirley nodded, placed the newly christened kitten Albedo in her box, and left the laboratory, wearing a smile the whole time.

The moment she left the laboratory, however, her smile disappeared as she turned her mind back to the holy ash. Sir Joseph had said that it appeared whenever the energy of the Pure World was siphoned and harnessed in their world. But it also appeared after the arms in the toilet disappeared, after the incident with Cutbush in the library, and most recently all over the washroom after the rats had vanished from sight.

That meant only one thing: that whatever had caused those horrific occurrences also came from the Pure World. Maybe it even came through to this world whenever the Eden Engine was fired up and the pure energy was siphoned off.

She had to find Griffin Avondale and tell him immediately.

Chapter Thirteen

The good news was, Albedo the kitten did not explode or otherwise suffer negative side effects. Quite the contrary, she proved to be quite gregarious. In the days following the second experiment, Shirley observed Albedo eat, play with string and wooden balls, explore the house (so long as Shirley was there to watch her explore), and napped. As far as Shirley knew, these were normal behaviors for cats and not signs that the energy of the pure world was disagreeing with her.

In addition, Albedo had grown rather attached to Shirley, and would only nap if curled up next to her mistress. Shirley found this behavior odd, as she understood cats to be rather standoffish, but she enjoyed being the object of Albedo's affection. It certainly made up for the bad news, which was that the staff at the Hunting Lodge's animosity towards her had risen considerably since Albedo had come into her care.

In all honesty, Shirley should have seen this coming. When she had first become Sir Joseph's assistant, after all, the staff had resented her and wondered if she had attained her new position by lying on her back. The gift of a kitten must have only confirmed their suspicions, and they had wasted no time in turning up their noses at her when they passed her in the halls or speaking to her as little as possible when forced to speak to her.

Lucky for her, their hostility had not bothered her. Shirley was an unsentimental person by nature, and even if she were not that way, she had not known any of the staff well enough to be upset by their behavior.

It had irked her, however, when both Nellie and Lucinda had approached her on Albedo's second night in her care, and had asked her, point-blank, if she were Sir Joseph's mistress or fiancée.

"No, I am not his mistress," Shirley had replied. "Nor am I his fiancée. I am his assistant, and that is it. The kitten was our latest test subject, so I'm taking care of her to make sure she doesn't get sick."

"You mean so it doesn't end up like that piglet I had to clean up a few weeks ago?" Nellie had asked. She then cupped her hands over her mouth, horrified. Shirley guessed that Nellie had been instructed not to speak of the piglet she had cleaned up and was now fearful for her position.

"Just like that," Shirley had answered. "And I won't tell Sir Joseph if you won't."

This had seemingly reassured both the girls, and they had spent a pleasant hour afterwards playing with Albedo and discussing anything that came to mind. Beneath all the smiles and discussion, however, she thought she sensed some slight apprehension from both of her only friends at the Lodge.

Imagine if they knew that Sir Joseph was calling me "my dear," she thought. *Or that he sometimes put his hand on my shoulder. They would never believe me, then.*

It was not as if she were lying to them, however. Not really. Sir Joseph held no romantic or sexual attraction towards her, she was certain of that. And she did not feel any romantic or sexual attraction towards him. Their relationship was entirely professional, a scientist and his assistant.

Except when he called her "my dear." And put a comforting hand on her shoulder. Then it felt—

Fatherly. Yes, that's what it is. That's what it has to be. He feels fatherly towards me.

Shirley had never met her own father. Nor did she know his name. Her mother had never spoken of him and asking about him would only make the poor woman shut her mouth and retreat deeper into the bottle than usual. And as knowing served Shirley no purpose, she had dropped the question quickly after realizing she would never find out.

Sir Joseph's kindness to her was what Shirley assumed a loving father displayed to his daughter. And she might have asked him if this was how he had acted to his own daughter, but he had shut himself up in the laboratory for the past several days, deep in research. He only emerged to pull meals on a tray inside with him and then put the trays out again when he was finished. Not even Shirley could get in to see him. The last time she had tried, the baronet had told her, quite plainly, not to disturb him unless there was some new development with Albedo or someone's life was at stake. She had not spoken to him since.

And so, life had gone on. Shirley monitored and played with the cat. Most of the staff ignored her or glared at her. Sir Joseph continued whatever research he needed to do alone. Nellie and Lucinda regularly talked with Shirley, and she with them.

The only thing out of the ordinary was that Shirley was seeing less and less of Griffin Avondale, usually only at supper, and even then, he was abnormally quiet. That was, until the first of August rolled around.

Shirley stood at the top of the stairs leading to the kitchen, waiting for Albedo to take her first steps on her own. The kitten, now around twelve weeks old and much larger than when she had emerged from the bombardment chamber, walked back and forth on the lip of the staircase, as if trying to ascertain what it was. She reached out a tentative paw, placed it on the next step, and then jumped down. Smiling, Shirley joined her on the next step and waited for Albedo to take the next one.

This continued for a while, until finally Albedo, who up until today had refused to go up and down stairs unless in someone's arms, reached the bottom of the stairs and stepped into the kitchen of her own accord. Shirley clapped as she joined Albedo in the kitchen. "Good girl, Albedo," she said, bending down to scratch the cat behind her ears. "I'm proud of you."

"What did she do?" Shirley glanced up as Nellie emerged from the cellar with a turkey carcass in her arms. She laid the carcass in a large pot and pulled some onions and potatoes out of a drawer.

"Hello Nellie," said Shirley. "Where's Mr. Garland and Luke?"

"They're on holiday," Nellie explained. "Gone off to Somerset for some sea and fresh air, I think. I'll be working the kitchens until they get back week after next." From the grin on her face, it was only too apparent that Nellie was happy to take over the kitchen duties. "But what did Albedo do that has you so proud?"

"She went down the stairs all by herself," Shirley informed her.

"Well, for walking down the stairs, here's a treat." Nellie threw a piece of turkey to the floor, which Albedo pounced on immediately and began to tear apart. As the cat enjoyed her meal, Shirley joined Nellie at the stove and asked her if anything exciting was happening lately.

"Not really," Nellie admitted. "I got a letter from my brother about this lass he was planning on marrying. Turns out she's run off with some musician to Dorset. Good riddance, I say. All that one cared about was what people would say about her looks. Lucinda has gone to London for the day. She's grown a few centimeters, and will need new clothes when she comes out of full mourning. And Mr. Avondale has gone down to the village—"

"Wait, what was that?"

"Mr. Avondale's gone down to the village," Nellie repeated. "About an hour ago. I heard him telling Mr. Milverton in case anyone was looking for him."

"Which village?" Shirley asked.

"The Closer Village. Why?"

Shirley did not answer. Instead, she handed Albedo to Nellie, told her she would be back soon, and ran out the kitchen.

***

The Closer Village was a small but pretty collection of houses and businesses grouped around a main road laid with stone and a memorial to the men from the village who had died in the Americas. Apparently, a total of seventeen locals had given their lives against Washington and his rebels. The village's biggest attraction, however, was a tall church of wood painted white sitting on a foundation of stone that had been painted white as well, which itself sat on a hill within the village that raised it above the other buildings. Walking around the church, one could see every house and person in the village clearly, so it was here that Shirley headed first when she did not immediately see Griffin upon entering.

From the village's northwest side, she glanced towards the square and the war memorial. While there were plenty of people around, none of them were Griffin Avondale. She tried the northeast, and once again did not see her quarry. The same for her the southeast and southwest sides. Annoyed and disappointed, she returned to the northwest side and sat on the church stoop to consider where Griffin might be and what she should do next.

It was entirely possible that she had missed him. Indeed, he may have returned to the Lodge while she had been rushing over. Or he could have gone over to the Further Village, which was smaller and did not have a great church overlooking it but was still quite scenic and serene.

Of course, there was always the possibility that Griffin had gone to London with Lucinda to chaperone her. A young lady did need her escort, after all. But if he went there, then what was the point of lying to Milverton? It was not as if going with Lucinda was scandalous or anything—

And then she spotted him, stepping out of the village's only tearoom and dressed for a leisurely day out. Shirley's spirit rose and she stood up. Now there was no escaping her. She would catch him and—

She stopped as she saw who he was with. It was the dark-haired girl from the garden party who had been so enamored of Griffin. Victoria something-or-other. And she was wearing another bright-red dress and hat, the kind a lady of high station wore to look her best in front of a prospective suitor.

Griffin had been courting her. That was why he had been avoiding her. He had been busy courting this young lady closer to his own station than Shirley was.

Perhaps I was able to drive him off after all, Shirley thought, oddly despondent now. Why, she could not say and she did not care. She turned and left the village as fast as she could, heading southeast and back to the Lodge. All thoughts of telling Griffin about the strange happenings in the Hunting Lodge and their connections to the Pure World had left her.

Right now, all she wanted was to get home to Albedo and forget everything for a while.

When the knock came on her door, Shirley had been napping on the bed, Albedo curled up against her belly. She sat up and called out, "Come in," in a sleep-riddled voice. The door opened and Griffin Avondale walked in. Shirley blinked and rubbed her eyes. She had been expecting Nellie or Lucinda, people she could afford to see her just coming out of sleep. Quickly she sat up straight, threw her legs over the side of the bed and stood up. On the bed, Albedo let out a petulant mewl, as if she could not believe Shirley had dared to disturb her nap.

"I was not expecting you, Mr. Avondale," Shirley said, sounding stiffer than usual. "What can I do for you?"

"I feel like I should ask you that question," he replied. "Were you looking for me in the village?"

"How did you know that? Did Nellie tell you?"

"I haven't seen Nellie since I returned. No, it was Reverend Fletcher. He saw you on the church steps and told me after you left. So, what was it you wanted to find me about?"

Shirley inhaled. Now was the time. She could discuss with Griffin the strange occurrences and their connection to the Pure World. Together, they might be able to get to the bottom of the mystery of what was happening in the Hunting Lodge.

But what came out of her mouth had no connection to the Pure World or the strange occurrences.

"I do not see how it is important anymore. It cannot compare to the importance of Victoria."

Anger and confusion rose onto Griffin's face. "I thought you wanted me to stop courting you. And why are you upset? Are you jealous?"

The question took Shirley by surprise. *Am I jealous?* she wondered. No sooner had she thought it, however, than she had the answer: she was jealous. Only a little jealous, but yes, she was jealous. But should she tell Griffin that?

Before she could consider how best to respond, Griffin continued speaking. "In any case, the subject of Victoria and me is now moot. She came today to tell me she could no longer visit with me or I with her. She even had to lie to her parents and say she was going to see a friend in Lavender Hill just to tell me."

"No longer visit?" Shirley repeated, incredulous. "Why?"

"Why not?" he scoffed. "I don't know if you've noticed, but Lucinda and I are dependent on our uncle, who seems unlikely to pass his title and all that comes with it to me upon his death. My finances are meager and I will not be returning to Oxford next month."

"You did what?" Shirley was aghast. Griffin, Lucinda and their parents had been so proud of his acceptance at Oxford. Deciding not to go must have been a difficult decision for him and must have made him feel he was letting his family down.

"What was I supposed to do?" Griffin asked, his tone even. "I would be penniless before I had finished the term. The only chance I have is to invest or marry and hope either opportunity proves lucrative.

Victoria's father is a baron, and while he is not opposed to the idea of a member of the gentry marrying his youngest daughter, he's opposed to one who cannot afford to give her the life worthy of a noble lady, let alone one whose future is based on mere chance. And as much as Victoria fancies me, she is terrified of what might happen if she defies her father and continues to allow a penniless orphan court her. Hence why we will no longer see each other."

"Oh," said Shirley. "I'm sorry to hear that." She meant it too, even if she applauded the two young lovers for putting practicality over sentiment or desire.

All her sympathy vanished in an instant, however, at Griffin's next words. "Why do you even care about whom I court? As I understand it, my uncle places you very highly above all the other women in this house. Including my sister!"

A flaming rage surged forth in Shirley's breast at the implication of his words. "I'll have you know, I am his assistant, and nothing more!" she hissed. "How dare you suggest that I—!"

"Then what about the cat?" Griffin asked, pointing to Albedo. The kitten licked her paws while watching them with her big, blue eyes, as if this were a confusing but entertaining show just for her enjoyment.

Shirley groaned. "She's a test subject I'm watching over," she answered. "Yes, I think Sir Joseph intends for her to be a gift for me, and I happily accepted her—"

"Ha! See!"

"—but I assure you, the intent was not to court me or to...do anything improper."

"Then what was it?" Griffin growled.

"I-I don't know!" Shirley admitted in a raised voice. "I want to say a father's love for his daughter, but I don't know what that's like. All I have to go on was your father's love towards Lucinda! And I am not exactly sure if that was standard for most fathers or the exception."

Griffin stared at her. "Like a...father's love...for his daughter?" he repeated.

Shirley shrugged. "I think so." With a sigh, she sat down on the bed again. Albedo padded over to her and slipped into her lap so Shirley could scratch her ears. She obliged the cat's wishes, albeit absentmindedly. "I don't know what else to call it. I know it is closer than just two people with a common goal, but at the same time, it's not indecent in any way. Not like what you're thinking."

"I wasn't—I mean...what are you two working on anyway?" Griffin asked after some flustered stammering. "What keeps you both so busy that you spend all day in that laboratory of his?"

Finally, something a little less complicated, Shirley thought with relief. And it gave her an inroad to discuss the strange appearances in the Lodge. Of course, Sir Joseph would be upset with her if he found out she had spoken to Griffin without permission, but given that every occurrence had threatened her life, she felt she could get away with speaking out of turn.

Before she could open her mouth, however, there was a scream in the hallway. Right outside Shirley's bedroom.

Griffin glanced behind him to the hallway. Even with his face turned away from her, Shirley could tell what he was thinking.

"Stay here," he instructed, running out of the room and towards whatever had uttered the scream. Shirley followed him out, her curiosity and worry overriding her caution. She pulled to a stop, however, as she saw Griffin leaning over the sill of one of the open windows. Fearing the worst, Shirley pushed him over and glanced downwards.

"Oh my God," she whispered, horrified. Lying on the ground two stories below was Nellie, her body lying on the grass below, one arm and both legs bent at odd angles.

Without waiting, Shirley ran downstairs and jumped out the first window she could find before sprinting to Nellie's side.

"Nellie!" Shirley cried. "Nellie, what happened? Somebody call a doctor! Nellie! What happened?"

The younger girl moaned and turned her head weakly towards Shirley. "Did it work?" she asked weakly.

"Did what work?" Shirley replied, her voice breaking. "Nellie, did what work?"

Nellie moaned again and mumbled something Shirley only partially caught. "...better. He said...better..."

"Oh my word," said a familiar voice. Griffin, Milverton, Mrs. Preston, and Hilly and Beth had finally arrived, their faces framed with horror.

"What are you just standing around there for?" Shirley sobbed. "Get help!"

Griffin and Milverton jumped as if startled, before rushing off in the direction of the village. Shirley watched them go before turning her attention back to Nellie. "Don't worry, Nellie," she whispered. "Mr. Avondale and Mr. Milverton have gone to get the village doctor. You'll be better soon."

"Yes," Nellie murmured, struggling to keep her uneven pupils focused on Shirley. "I'll be...better."

Suddenly Nellie sat up straight and opened her mouth. Black vomit spewed forth from her, staining her dress and apron. Hilly and Beth screamed in horror and disgust, while Mrs. Preston bent over to be sick as well. Shirley only watched in horror as she realized that the black vomit was in truth normal vomit mixed with blood.

Nellie swayed back and forth for a moment. Then, as sores appeared on her cheeks and forehead and began to seep blood, she fell back and into unconsciousness.

Chapter Fourteen

Mix the ingredients for a Gugelhupf cake. Water, dry yeast, milk, butter, sugar, flour, salt, eggs, golden raisins, ground orange peel and crushed almonds. Pour the batter into the mold. Place the mold into the oven. Start to work on the bread. Take the cake out of the oven at the right time and place it on the cooling rack. Put the bread on a tray and place the tray into the oven. Start to work on the chocolate cake while Gugelhupf cake cools. Cocoa powder, flour, eggs, sugar, milk, water...

Shirley did all these actions mechanically, trying to focus on the work and not think of the black band she wore around her arm now, or whom that black band represented. When she had first started working as a maid, one of the maids she had worked with had said that when she was upset, she should bake, if only to get her mind off whatever was making her upset. "That, and it'll put you on the master's good side," she had said. "Nobody can resist a good cake or tart, mark my words."

Shirley did not get upset often, at least not as upset that she needed something to take her mind off her misery. But the few times she had become that upset, baking had proved helpful in calming her mood and giving her an outlet to channel her feelings.

Until now, that was. Until last night.

The doctor from the Closer Village had been summoned, but he could offer nothing for Nellie. The matter of her broken limbs aside, he could find no explanation for either the sores appearing over her body or why she was vomiting blood. In the end, all he could do was prescribe morphine for the pain and tell Shirley and Mrs. Preston to make Nellie as comfortable as possible.

So, they had waited, bandaged up the sores as best as possible, and tried to make her more comfortable. As the sun had begun to set, Lucinda had arrived home and, after having been informed by

Griffin of what had happened, had rushed down to Nellie's room in the basement to hold vigil with Shirley and Mrs. Preston.

But what really broke Shirley's heart, more than anything else, was that Nellie actually woke up and became lucid for a minute. Shirley had not noticed the poor girl stirring, but Lucinda had. She had jumped up from her kneeling position next to the bed and had almost grabbed Nellie's hand before remembering that the arm the hand was attached to was broken. Instead, she grabbed and squeezed Shirley's hand and asked, "How are you feeling?"

For a moment, the only sound Nellie made was a moaning noise, the kind an invalid made when trying to gather the energy to speak. Finally, she whispered, "You're both here. I'm glad."

The sound of her voice was almost too much for Shirley, and she squeezed Lucinda's hand back. "Nellie, what happened to you?" she asked. "Why did you fall out the window? Why are you...why are you—?"

She could not bring herself to finish that sentence, however, and instead settled for holding back her tears and taking the hand that was unbroken in her free one. The fingers that encircled her own were weak and fragile, with none of the strength belonging to a maid used to hard work from sunup to well past sundown. Nellie made that horrible moaning noise again and whispered, "I was waiting for you both to be here. I was waiting...for my friends."

Tears fell down Lucinda's face and landed on the blankets. "What do you mean? Why were you waiting for us?"

"I'm sorry," she said, her every breath a gasp for more oxygen. "I wish we could have had ice cream together again."

Nellie closed her eyes and lay back against the pillow. The fingers holding Shirley's hand went limp. And, even as her mind tried to deny reality, Shirley let the tears flow. Beside her, Lucinda wailed.

That had been the night before. Nellie's funeral would be in three days, once a coffin had been built and a hole dug for it in the Closer

Village's graveyard. Sir Joseph had been charitable enough to offer to pay for everything and to let Nellie's family stay in the Lodge when they arrived in two days hence. He had actually come out of the laboratory this morning, looking quite haggard after being sealed off in the laboratory this whole time, to make that announcement. Shirley had been so touched by the baronet's thoughtful gesture, she had nearly hugged him right there and then in the dining room. The only thing that had kept her from doing so had not been any sort of propriety between employer and employee, but the desire not to give the rest of the staff a reason to gossip.

Still, Sir Joseph's gesture did not lessen any of her pain. Nor did baking all these cakes and breads and treats. She had baked enough pastries to fill the shelves of a bakery, but she was in more pain than she had ever been in her life, in more pain than when her mother had died. Shirley had loved Nellie. The girl had been like a younger sister to her, and now she was gone. She was gone, and what was the point of baking all these sweets? They would all go to waste, they would not lessen anyone's grief, let alone her own. She—!

"What the hell?" Griffin exclaimed as he walked into the kitchen. He had arrived just in time to see Shirley throw a bowl of flour at the wall. The flour went everywhere as the bowl clattered on the ground. He then turned his attention to her, and before Shirley could stop him, had wrapped her in his embrace. She wanted to struggle out of his grip, but then the tears began again and she accepted the gesture.

"I'm so sorry," he whispered. "I know you two were close."

"We were both close to her," she said. "Lucinda and I."

"I know," Griffin replied. "She's been grieving hard for Nellie as well. I think even Uncle Joseph is trying to help her. He even invited her into his laboratory to talk."

"Sir Joseph did that?" Despite her pain, Shirley managed a small smile. "He does care for you both, it seems."

"It would seem so. I did not think it was possible, but maybe he feels something for us beyond family responsibility."

They stood in silence for a while. When Shirley's tears had dried up, she coughed and said, "You can let me go. I'm fine now."

"No, you're not," he replied. "You're not fine."

"Well, you should stop holding me," Shirley reminded him. "Someone might see us and make a strange assumption. And when you're trying to find an acceptable bride—"

"Shirley, haven't you realized it by now?" Griffin interrupted. "Yesterday's meeting with Victoria was the final nail. I am no longer acceptable amongst upper-class families. I no longer have to force myself to court them just because society says I must."

Shirley glanced up at his face, confused. "What?"

"I said my position in society is no longer too high for you," Griffin explained. "I'm just the son of the deceased president of a drill company. Someone who was unable to hold onto his father's company and who has only a meager sum left in the bank. Nothing more, nothing less."

At once, Shirley understood the importance of what he was saying. Of what Griffin was implying could now be possible for them. At once, a million thoughts and emotions swept through her, each fighting for dominance as she tried to figure out how to respond. In the end, it was the wise and practiced voice of her practical mind that won out.

"If you think that's going to get me to marry you, you have another think coming," she replied. "I refuse to marry anyone who cannot provide an income for me. And you said it yourself, your funds are meager."

Griffin opened his mouth to reply. But before he could get a word out, a new, heavy, rasping breath scuttled forth through the kitchen.

"Did I hear that right, Griffin? Are you lowering yourself for the likes of her?"

Griffin and Shirley started and broke apart, searching the room for the source of the voice. At the same time, all the electric lights in the kitchen went out, save for one in the far back. It let out a soft halo of light, beyond which was complete and total darkness. The hairs on the back of Shirley's neck rose as she realized what was happening. "Oh no," she whispered. Then louder, "Griffin, into the light!"

Even as she said it, however, Griffin was backing under the sconce with her. From the other end of the kitchen came shuffling footsteps.

"*Griffin, you stupid, stupid boy,*" said the raspy voice. "*I raised you for more than this. I raised you to be more than what I was. I raised you to reach for the highest tiers of society. And you want to lower yourself to some strumpet maid? A drunk's bastard whelp from Whitechapel with an ugly eye?*"

Something about that voice sounded familiar to Shirley. She glanced at Griffin and observed how wide and terrified his eyes were. "You cannot be here," he said, his voice weak and trembling. "I saw you into the ground! I saw you lowered myself!"

"*Griffin, I may be dead, but I am not gone,*" said the voice. A figure stepped forward, just beyond the edge of the light, and glared at them. "*I'm your father, boy. I will always be with you.*"

Shirley inhaled. It was no wonder she had recognized that voice. She had worked for the owner of that voice for almost a year.

Mr. Avondale stepped into the light. While he had been a reasonably handsome man in life, now he appeared before them in death with gray skin covering a twisted and broken body, his head cocked at an unnatural angle on his neck. One eye was missing from its orb and the other focused on them with hatred and contempt.

"*I sacrificed so much for you,*" said the revenant. "*I worked myself to the bone! And you squandered every opportunity I gave you. You failed me at Eton! You deferred from Oxford! And now you want to give up any chance of advancement just to have your way with this slut! You know she's sleeping with your uncle!*"

"Don't you dare talk about her like that!" Griffin roared, suddenly angry. "You don't know her! Not like I do!"

"You *don't know her!*" The revenant yelled, leaping forward and bridging the distance between them. With a gnarled hand, he reached out and grabbed Griffin by the throat, lifting him into the air. "*You don't know what strumpets like her will do. What they will say and do for a bit of coin! I'd rather see you join me in the grave before you waste your life on her!*"

"Let him go!" Shirley yelled. She pulled her arm back to punch him, but then a hand grabbed her fist and spun her around. There, his eyes wild with rage and insanity, stood Thomas Hayne Cutbush, covered in the blood of Mary Jane Kelly. Shirley's insides went cold as he pulled her towards him, his strength monstrous.

"*Am I hearing that right, girl?*" he growled, his breath rancid. It filled her nostrils along with the scent of blood, hot and coppery. Shirley gagged and whimpered; once again, she was ten years old and unable to escape from the monster in human form as he turned what had once been a living woman into a grotesque piece of art dedicated to his own delusions. "*Are you poisoning that boy? Making him want you so you can do as you please to him? Well, we can't have that.*"

With his free hand, Cutbush reached into his coat and pulled out a butcher's knife covered in dried blood. Shirley screamed, only to cry out as she was pushed with terrific force into the wall. Laughing cruelly, Cutbush pressed the knife against her throat. She flinched at its cold touch.

"*I'll have to rip you up, little girl,*" Cutbush informed her. "*I warned you this would happen. But you didn't listen!*"

Shirley cried out as the knife dug a little into her neck and blood dribbled out. Tears spilled down her cheeks as she gazed at Cutbush's face. *So, this is how I end*, she thought sorrowfully. *As Jack the Ripper's sixth victim.* She closed her eyes and waited for the inevitable.

There was a loud, high-pitched war-cry from the darkness. Shirley opened her eyelids just in time to see a frying pan whizz through the air towards Cutbush's head. Yet even as it made contact, Cutbush's head dissolved, followed by the rest of his body. The knife he was holding fell to the ground, clattered against the tile, and then blew apart like dust.

Like holy ash.

Shirley glanced from where the knife had fallen to the frying pan, and saw Mrs. Preston holding it and pulling back for another strike, this time for Mr. Avondale. The revenant, however, reached up and grabbed the pan in his free hand on the downward strike. It laughed as Mrs. Preston's eyes went from furious to fearful.

Acting on instinct, Shirley rushed forward and punched Mr. Avondale in the neck. It must have been a stronger tap than she had thought, because he released both Griffin and the frying pan and wheeled back, clutching his throat in his hands and making a strange, choking noise. A moment later, however, he lowered his hands and balled them into fists.

"*You little wench!*" he hissed. "*I'll make you regret that!*"

The Mr. Avondale-revenant rushed forward with a guttural roar. Shirley yelped and braced for the impact of a fist.

"Don't you touch her!" Griffin yelled. Bounding forward, he bent low and tackled his father around the waist. Mr. Avondale uttered a squawk of surprise before he was slammed into a rack of pots and pans. Several utensils fell from the rack, landing on and around them. Griffin grabbed one of them before it hit the ground, a steak mallet, and brought it swinging upwards into the revenant's temple.

There was a squelching noise as the mallet passed through the rotting skin and into Mr. Avondale's skull. The corpse's mouth dropped open in surprise and it let out a sound like a death rattle. Then it began to dissolve, starting from the wound the steak mallet had made and spreading outward. A moment later, Griffin was pinning nothing but empty air as motes of ash wheeled through the air.

With the destruction of the Mr. Avondale revenant, the rest of the lights flickered back on. All three of them blinked as their eyes adjusted. When they could see again, Mrs. Preston sighed and placed the pan on the island before saying in her thickest Midlands accent, "I guess you two now know about the stranger problems of the Hunting Lodge. Is this your first time experiencing them, or have you known for a while?"

Chapter Fifteen

Shirley waited to satisfy her curiosity until they were out of the kitchen and seated in one of the parlors. While Mrs. Preston placed disinfectant and a bandage on her neck, Shirley sucked in a deep breath and said, "You seem to know much about what that was down there."

"So do you," Mrs. Preston replied. "That day you screamed and fell out of that water closet, you weren't screaming over a spider, were you, dearie? You saw something in there, something you couldn't explain, and you lied to keep your job."

"So, what is it?" Griffin asked, his voice slightly hoarse. He rubbed the red marks around his neck tenderly. His tie was loosened and the top buttons of his shirt had been undone so he could breathe easier. "What are those...visions, I guess you could call them."

"I wish I knew," Mrs. Preston replied. "They just started showing up three or four years ago, around the time Sir Joseph started building whatever that giant machine in the ballroom is. I think everyone but Sir Joseph has seen something at one point or another, something that scares them to the very core of their beings. They wouldn't be harmed or nothing, but some of the staff were scared so bad, they left."

"You mean not everyone left because Sir Joseph cut the staff?" Shirley asked as Mrs. Preston drew away from her neck.

"That's right. Had three maids and a footman quit on us. Said they could no longer work in a house that's haunted."

"Why did you keep it a secret?" Griffin raged. He coughed, then resumed, "Why did you not tell someone?"

"Tell someone what?" asked Mrs. Preston. "That the Lodge was haunted? That people were seeing whatever scared them the most? Working for the baronet is hard enough! His scandals touched us too, you know. Made it more difficult for those of us who left to find new positions. If we added ghost stories to the Lodge's reputation, we would never find reputable employment! Besides, the spirits or whatever never attacked anyone before. Mostly they scared us. Granted, that was bad enough, but at least we could live with it."

"Well, they're attacking us now," Griffin replied. "And I'm sure they're aiming to murder us."

"I have noticed, Mr. Avondale," said Mrs. Preston. "Which is why I'm planning on leaving after we've laid poor Ms. Dean to rest and heading to stay with my daughter in Bedfordshire. Mr. Milverton and the other maids are planning to leave as well. It's unfortunate. The Lodge has been my home since Sir Joseph was a boy, but it's not worth dying over. Hopefully, whatever these things are will leave us alone until then. I don't know about you, dearies, but I do not want to be murdered by the Black Shuck. As I'm sure you don't want to be murdered by your father, Mr. Avondale. Or you don't want to be murdered by—who attacked you, dearie?"

"Jack the Ripper," Shirley replied. "I met him when I was a girl."

Mrs. Preston gazed at Shirley as if to determine if she was lying. When she realized Shirley was being truthful, she whispered, "My word. Then you definitely should vacate this place as soon as possible."

Shirley ignored her and turned to Griffin. "Was your father always like that?" she asked. "When you were alone with him, I mean?"

Griffin shook his head. "But I feared that was what he thought of me. That I was never good enough for his standards. I'm certain my love for you would never have met his approval. I guess whatever attacked us knew that somehow and used it against me."

"If it helps, I only ever heard him praise you when he spoke of you."

"Thank you. It does."

"Well, if you two do not need me anymore," Mrs. Preston interrupted, "I will take my leave. I still have much to pack before I go—!"

"Not just yet," Shirley said, holding up a finger. She could almost hear her thoughts with her ears, like the gears of a great machine, making connections between the strange apparitions they had encountered and something Mrs. Preston had said earlier. "You said all these things started showing up around the time Sir Joseph started working on the Eden Engine?"

"That's right," Mrs. Preston replied. "But I don't see what one has to do with the other. It's only a machine, after all. It can't do that much, can it? Also, it's called the Eden Engine?"

"Shirley, what are you thinking?" Griffin asked. "Does my uncle's machine have something to do with all this?"

"I think it does," she answered. "Have for a while now, really. But what you said, Mrs. Preston, gives me more proof."

Briefly, she explained Plato's Theory of Forms to them, mostly for the benefit of Mrs. Preston, who was unfamiliar with it. She then revealed the purpose of the Eden Engine, and how the energy of the Pure World produced the same ash that appeared after each of the strange occurrences.

When she was done, Griffin had a stricken look on his face. Something had occurred to him.

"You said Uncle Joseph's machine can reach the Pure World?" he asked. "A world where the perfect, purest idea of everything exists as reality?"

"That's right," Shirley replied.

"Even the purest idea of terror?"

Shirley felt the blood drain from her face. "Oh my God," she whispered.

Suddenly, it all made sense. Something that could take the form of anyone's worst fear. Something from the Pure World, where everything was perfect and unsullied.

"Pure Terror," Griffin said. "Uncle Joseph's been stealing energy from that world. Maybe when he does, the Idea of Terror comes through as well and looks for anyone to terrify. Then after a while, it goes back, and waits for the Eden Engine to steal more energy."

"But why?" asked Mrs. Preston. "Why is Terror coming through? Why could Pure Happiness not come through? Or Pure Music, or something else we would be happy to have come through?"

"Who knows?" Shirley wondered aloud, her mind running through the possibilities. "Who knows how things work over in the Pure World? It might only be coming over here accidentally. It might not even be aware of what's happening. It's just doing what it's supposed to do, which is to terrify anyone it encounters."

"Accident or not, we have to warn Uncle Joseph," said Griffin. "Before he fires up that Engine again and lets the Terror through again."

"Come along, Mrs. Preston!" Shirley stood and turned towards the door. "We have to let Sir Joseph know what's going on."

"Wait, I already told you—fine! Wait for me!"

They rushed from the parlor, across the foyer and into the north wing. As the laboratory approached, however, Shirley heard a familiar noise coming from behind the closed doors. A terrible cacophony of spinning gears, clanging levers, and humming consoles.

"He's turned the Engine on!" Shirley yelled, wrenching open the doors. "We have to stop him!"

They ran into the laboratory, Griffin and Mrs. Preston following behind Shirley as she led them to Console Seven. When they arrived, they found Sir Joseph standing by the bombardment chamber, which was full of pure white light. He turned to them and flashed them a wide, insane smile.

"Ah, Shirley. Griffin. Mrs. Preston. You are just in time. I think I'm close to perfecting the process for humans."

"Sir, you need to shut the Engine down!" Shirley shouted, terrified.

"Quite right, my dear," he replied, as calm as could be. He flipped the switch up into the off position. "Come now. Help me turn the machine off."

Shirley and Sir Joseph ran between the consoles, turning the Engine off. When the noise had died down, Shirley had time to wonder about what Sir Joseph had said. *I think I'm close to perfecting the process for humans.* Who did he put into the bombardment chamber?

"Lucinda!"

Shirley started as Griffin shouted and spun around. The light in the bombardment chamber was dissipating. And beyond the dirty glass stood Lucinda Avondale, looking pale and dazed.

Chapter Sixteen

With a cry of horror, Griffin pushed past Sir Joseph and unlocked the bombardment chamber. Lucinda fell out with a moan into her brother's waiting arms, having apparently fainted. Panicking, he pulled her away from the bombardment chamber and to the other end of the laboratory. Shirley and Mrs. Preston rushed to join him, while Sir Joseph took his time, as if he were on a leisurely stroll through a public park.

Laying her on the ground, Griffin shook Lucinda's shoulders and patted her cheeks. The whole time he called her name and begged her to wake up. After a moment, Lucinda groaned and opened her eyes.

"Griffin?" she said. "What happened?"

"You went through the purification process in the Eden Engine, remember?" said Sir Joseph, standing by a workbench. "You said you wanted to be a perfect lady, one all of society would love. One who might even be able to land the heart of a prince."

"What?" Griffin roared, glancing between his sister and great-uncle. "You fed her that stack of lies? You made her believe that?"

"I did it for you," Lucinda revealed. All but Sir Joseph stared at her with shock and confusion. "I did it to help you."

"Oh my word," said Mrs. Preston.

"Why would you do that?" asked Shirley, barely keeping her tears and anxiety in check. She kept expecting Lucinda to explode, just as the little piglet had after its leg had grown into place.

"I cannot let my brother give up all his dreams," she replied, reaching a shaking hand up and cupping her brother's cheek. "He's already given up so much for me. This was how I could help him."

Griffin held her hand against his cheek, tears welling in his eyes. "Lucinda. You did not have to go to such lengths for me."

"Why are you crying?" she asked. "Be happy. My future husband will fund you if I ask him to, whether it be in business or in education.

He will help you marry Victoria, or any young lady you want. All because he will love me so, and all because of Uncle Joseph's kindness—argh!"

Lucinda winced and brought both her hands to her belly. Underneath the fabric of her dress, Shirley spotted what looked like hills rising out of her before receding back into her. "What's happening?" she asked.

"Nothing to worry about, Shirley, my dear," Sir Joseph assured her. "Just the changes taking place in Lucinda. She'll be a perfect society lady in no time at all."

But despite Sir Joseph's optimism, Lucinda did not seem to be improving. Instead, the rising and receding hills spread from her belly to her entire abdomen, to her limbs, and finally to her face. And the more they spread, the more in pain she seemed to be. When she finally burst out screaming, Griffin turned to Sir Joseph in desperation. "Do something!" he shouted.

Sir Joseph only shook his head. "It would appear that I was correct. The idea of a 'perfect lady' is so fraught and full of contradictions, that the pure energy cannot change her from her flawed self to that ideal being. I thought that might pose an obstacle, given my own wife could not find a balance between 'too many emotions' and 'being an unfeeling woman,' but I had to find out the Engine's limits. At the very least, I thought it was possible she would no longer need to defecate to rid herself of waste products."

"You bastard!" Griffin screamed. "You knew this would happen?"

"Sh-Shirley!" Lucinda muttered. Her screams had died down to moans as her skin shifted like the waves of a choppy lake.

Shirley knelt beside Lucinda and took her hand. "I'm here," she said. Terror had spread through every vein and artery of her body, making it difficult to think straight. "I'm here, Lucinda. What do you need?"

Despite what was happening to her and the pain she must have been feeling, Lucinda managed a smile. "I am so glad," she said, taking her brother's hand with her free one. "The people I love the most are here with me. I just wish..."

But whatever she wished for, they would never find out. Her voice faded, her eyes closed, and then Lucinda Avondale melted and dissolved into a puddle. Shirley and Griffin rose with horrified screams as what had been their friend and sister spread outwards from her dress, looking like the largest spill of cake batter ever. Shirley shook the liquid on her fingers off, realizing, with a disgusted thought, that she was shaking off her last real friend in the world.

Scooting around the spreading pool of what had been Lucinda to where Mrs. Preston and Griffin stood, she turned around to Sir Joseph and was appalled to see that he seemed totally unaffected by the death of his niece, let alone at the death caused by his own machine. What he said next only appalled her more.

"Such a shame. I was sure after the failure of that maid, I had perfected the process. But I guess more work is needed before I can try again on another live subject."

"Did you say you used the Engine on a maid?" she asked, horrified.

Sir Joseph nodded. "Yes, the Dean girl. Her failure to reach perfection showed me how to improve the Engine for humans, however, so her death was not a total waste. In any case, the next experiment should be a success. After all, what has to be accomplished is nowhere near as impossible as creating an impossible archetype."

Shirley felt her blood chill. Sinking to her knees, she finally let the tears she had been holding back loose. Sir Joseph had killed Nellie. He was the cause of her strange and sudden illness. He had used the Engine on her and then let her die in that horrible way. *How could he do this?*

"Another experiment?" Mrs. Preston asked in dismay. "Surely, Sir Joseph, you would not try this again?"

"You monster!" Griffin screamed, his voice choked with sobs. "Haven't you done enough? You don't even know what that machine is doing!"

Sir Joseph smiled madly at them. "On the contrary, I know exactly what it does. You see, the Pure World spoke to me recently. It spoke to *me*!" His insane smile grew wider as he continued, "You see, the Pure World is alive and intelligent and sentient! And it wants to help this imperfect world. It wants to bring the Garden of Eden back to our world!"

"Sir Joseph, you can't do that," Shirley interrupted.

The baronet's face fell and he turned to Shirley, still kneeling on the floor, in surprise. "Why is that, my dear? Did you not share my dream as well?"

"I did!" she replied. "I still do! But don't you see? The price isn't worth it!" She gestured behind her at what had been Lucinda Avondale up until a few moments ago. "Besides, you don't know what's been happening around the Lodge. The Engine has been letting something through. Something terrible!"

"Please, Sir Joseph!" Mrs. Preston begged. "Please listen to us and call off this foolish mission! There are things happening in the Lodge that I fear are endangering all our lives!"

Sir Joseph's face registered confusion for a moment. Then it morphed into anger as he said, "Foolish mission? I beg to differ."

Then he pulled a revolver out of his coat and fired two shots.

Shirley screamed and ducked down as the bullets roared over her head. When the gunshots had died away, she turned around and saw, to her horror, Mrs. Preston lying in what was left of Lucinda, a dribble of blood flowing from her forehead. A moan to her left alerted her to Griffin, who was lying on the ground and holding his knee. The bullet had shattered his kneecap.

"Damn," Sir Joseph murmured, pocketing the gun again. "The boy moved. Well, no matter. What is important is you, my dear."

Before Shirley could ask what he meant or try to get away, Sir Joseph had crossed to her, grabbed her arm and began dragging her towards the Eden Engine. Towards Console Seven and the bombardment chamber.

"No!" Shirley yelled in terror. She tried to free herself from the baronet's grip, but it was like trying to bend steel.

"I must admit, Shirley, since I first met you, I felt we had a connection," Sir Joseph said as he continued to pull her forward. "It only intensified when you began to work for me as my assistant. In time, I began to think of you like a daughter. But since we began the experiments on live subjects, I've been certain. And now, after what I've found out, I know for certain." He laughed madly. "You *are* my daughter, Shirley Dobbins! The blood that flows through your veins is the same as mine! And I will give my daughter, my own flesh and blood, the very best! No one will look down upon you again!"

He's gone mad, Shirley thought. *The Pure Terror spoke to him, not the Pure World, and now he's gone mad. Mad enough that he'll kill me!*

She struggled to break free, but it was as if trying to break free of gravity. Sir Joseph continued to pull her along, unmindful of her futile attempts. When they reached Console Seven, he tossed her into the bombardment chamber with as much ease as throwing a ragdoll. Shirley cried out, slid to the bottom of the chamber, and watched with mounting terror as Sir Joseph locked her into the chamber.

Scrambling to her feet, Shirley banged on the glass with her fists and screamed. Sir Joseph ignored her, running from console to console to turn the Engine on again. A cleansing burst of pure energy, golden and fragrant, hissed into the bombardment chamber, covering Shirley in golden light. She coughed as it entered her nostrils and mouth and then into her lungs like gas. Her body tingled uncomfortably as the glow dissipated.

Oh God, he's going to kill me! She pounded harder on the glass, screaming for Sir Joseph to let her out. The baronet only smiled and waved excitedly at her, like a parent waving at a child on a roundabout ride.

As the Engine roared to life and pure energy began to move through the vacuum tubes and consoles to Console Seven, Sir Joseph strolled to the bombardment chamber and put a hand on the final switch. He smiled and gave Shirley a knowing wink, though what she was supposed to know, she had no idea.

Suddenly a pair of arms tackled Sir Joseph and pulled him away from the switch. It was Griffin, his knee still shattered, but the rest of him raring for a fight. Shirley watched with trepidation as they struggled against each other, and then struggled for the revolver as Sir Joseph tried to pull it from his pocket again.

Suddenly, Sir Joseph freed his arms from Griffin's grip and attempted to raise the one holding the gun to eye level. Griffin raised his good leg into the air and, with a tortured scream, delivered a strong kick into his great-uncle's side. Sir Joseph fell to the ground and the revolver went flying into a corner. Crying out in agony, Griffin toppled over, but managed to pull himself up again and limp towards the bombardment chamber. Shirley watched, frozen, as he undid the latch and slid back the glass door.

"Griffin!" Shirley jumped out of the bombardment chamber and wrapped her arms around the injured young man. He cried out again but managed to stay standing, wrapping his own arms around Shirley. Silently, Shirley promised herself if they both managed to leave the Lodge, she would consider marrying him, income be damned.

She was pulled from her thoughts, however, as she noticed the level of noise coming from the Engine. She looked around, and saw that bright light was pushing through the steel plates that made up Console Seven. Something was wrong with the Engine.

"It doesn't matter if you stopped me!"

Shirley and Griffin turned to Sir Joseph, who had shakily gotten to his feet and stood with the second most horrible smile Shirley had ever seen on a human face. "It doesn't matter if you stopped me!" he repeated, somehow making himself heard over all the noise. "The process has already begun. Mankind will reach its destined perfection. Behold, the pure world comes!"

Console Seven exploded.

Chapter Seventeen

A blast of wind with the strength of a hurricane lifted Shirley, Griffin and the many workbenches and pieces of equipment not nailed down flying in every direction. With a cry of pain, Shirley landed on top of a pile of broken glass beakers and bottles, the glass lancing through her skin and into the meat of her back. Bleeding and in agony, she lifted herself off the ground and searched for Griffin. She found him lying a couple meters away, trapped underneath half a broken workbench.

"Griffin!" Despite the pain in her back, she ran to his side and attempted to pull the workbench off, but it was too heavy. Underneath the heavy planks of wood, Griffin moaned and pointed behind her.

"Look," he whispered, pointing back at Console Seven.

Shirley looked, and wished she had not.

The top of Console Seven looked like a volcano had exploded from within its shell. Beautiful white light spilled forth like lava, running down the sides of the machine in rivers and forming vast pools on the floor that spread outward and towards them. But it was what was rising out of the top of the machine like smoke and ash that terrified her: a huge, growing mass of darkness, of negative space, reaching towards the ceiling and spreading outwards. And within that negative space was something alive. Shirley sensed it with her mind. Something old, sentient, and malevolent. It was able to see without eyes, to hear without ears, and to think without a mind.

It was the Pure Terror, and it knew her fear.

"My God."

Shirley glanced to Sir Joseph, who stood leaning against Console Eleven, his clothes ragged and his hair in disarray. A long trail of blood ran down from his forehead and dripped off the edge of his cheeks, making his haggard appearance even more ghastly than before.

But it was the horror in his eyes that struck Shirley. *He's regained his sanity*, she thought. *He knows he's done something he should not have.*

And then Sir Joseph asked the obvious next question: "What have I done?"

No sooner had he finished speaking than the hazy outline of a figure appeared in front of him. Shirley and the baronet stared as the figure became defined and took on the appearance of Sir Joseph. Only this version was broken, twisted, bent, and full of hate. The Sir Joseph-copy glared at the real Sir Joseph, who shuffled back in terror.

"Everything you've ever done is a failure," the copy growled. "You have failed everyone who ever knew you. Especially your own children."

"No!" Sir Joseph cried. "I-I did not! I did this for them!"

"And yet you still failed your only living child." The copy gestured at Shirley.

Sir Joseph and Shirley's eyes connected, and she saw tears were welling up in his.

"Forgive me, my dear," he said. "I should have told you the moment I realized. And I never should have brought you into this—!"

Before he could finish apologizing, the copy reached out, grabbed Sir Joseph by the chin and back of the head, and twisted. Shirley winced as Sir Joseph's neck made a sickening crack, and then watched as he fell to the floor, his eyes glassy and trapped forever in an expression of apology. The twisted copy of Sir Joseph smiled wickedly before dissolving in a cloud of holy ash.

Despite all the crying she had done lately, Shirley felt fresh tears spring to her eyes and her chest seize with pain. Once more, she had lost someone important to her. Only she had not realized how important he was until it was too late. Whether or not he had been her father like he claimed, Sir Joseph had been like a father to her. And now, like Nellie and Lucinda, he had died right before her very eyes.

"What on Earth is happening—my word!"

By the doors to the laboratory, Milverton, Hilly and Beth had arrived, and were staring at the Eden Engine and what was rising out of it with abject horror. Shirley felt her heart skip a beat as she realized what would happen if they stayed any longer.

"Run!" she screamed. All three heads turned to face her, shock and confusion mixing with their terror. "Run! Before it kills you too!"

"My goodness, is that Sir Joseph?" Milverton shouted, pointing at the baronet's body.

"He's dead!" Hilly yelled.

Beth crossed herself. "Lord protect us."

From the depths of the negative space, something let out a noise that reverberated through the laboratory and in Shirley's head. She winced as the noise, something between a roar and a foghorn, shook her skeleton and her mental equilibrium. A second later, three forms rocketed out of the darkness and towards Milverton and the maids. One was of an old woman with a rolling pin; another was a spider as big as a mastiff, with long legs and giant fangs dripping with venom; and the third was of a woman wearing a blue robe and veil, anger literally flaming out of her eyes as she pointed forward with one accusatory arm and held a flaming sword aloft with another.

Milverton, Hilly and Beth spotted the two women and the spider and let out horrified screams. They immediately turned and ran out of the laboratory, while the women and the spider, their worst fears, chased after them.

"*Terrifying, isn't it?*"

Shirley jumped as Cutbush and the revenant of Mr. Avondale appeared before her and Griffin, satisfied smirks on their faces.

"Y-You're not real," she stammered.

"*But we are*," said Cutbush. Somewhere in the back of her mind, Shirley realized she was speaking not to the image of Cutbush but to the older, more primal entity that had created the image. To the Pure Terror itself. "*We are very real. We have always been real. And we shall always be real.*"

"*And this world is so new and beautiful in its ugliness,*" the revenant added, again speaking for the force that had created it. "*So full of fears. We will ride forth and fill this world with their fears. It will be glorious.*"

"*And now that our pawn is dead,*" they said in unison, gesturing at Sir Joseph, "*no one can send us back!*"

Shirley's mind filled with horrible visions. Whether they had been placed in her head by the monsters in front of her, or they had risen organically from her own imagination, she could not say. Whatever their origin, they were vivid and terrible: London on fire as people ran from their own worst nightmares; the countryside full of families and military forces fleeing the carnage, only to be slaughtered by the thousands as their fears manifested from above and fell upon them; and a black cloud of negative space floating over the British Isles, sending out its avatars of terror towards the continent and America to wreak further havoc.

Shirley's chest tightened with panic. *I can't let that happen.*

"*But it will happen,*" Cutbush and the revenant promised her, still speaking in unison. "*It will happen, and you cannot stop it.*"

Trying her best to ignore their voices, Shirley's eyes darted around, looking for something—*anything!*—that she could use to stop the Pure Terror. She could not turn the Engine off, not as it was now, but if she could just find another way to keep the Terror from leaving the Lodge—

And then she spotted Sir Joseph's revolver lying at the foot of Console One. And an idea formed crystal-clear in her mind. It was perfect.

Out of the corner of her eye, Shirley caught the glint of a knife being raised. The Cutbush image was going to stab her.

With a cry, Shirley jumped and dodged the descending knife. She rolled across the ground, over the broken glass again, and came to a stop a few paces from the doors. Ignoring the pain, she rushed to her feet and ran towards the Engine and the revolver.

"*No*!" screamed Cutbush and the revenant. The figure of Cutbush manifested between Shirley and the Engine, its knife held high. Shirley bent as she ran and, elbow out in front of her, rammed the figure in the stomach.

"You're not him!" she screamed. "You're just a bad copy!"

The Cutbush figure fell to the ground with a groan of pain. Shirley jumped over it and scooped up the revolver. Then she ran at full speed to Console Seven, dodging the Mr. Avondale-revenant as it tried to scoop her up in its arms and stop her. When she was close enough, she dove into the glowing lake of pure energy that had formed at the base of the console, one thought in her head.

Make it the ultimate killing machine. And make me strong enough to wield it and get out of here.

She landed in the thick of the glowing white light and immediately felt a change overcome her body. The pure energy swirled around her and into her, clearing all the glass and debris and infections from her wounds before healing them. Even the bandage on her neck fell away as the wound sealed itself, leaving behind only perfect skin. At the same time, a vortex of energy swirled around the revolver like a tornado, causing the metal to glow and shimmer.

Reenergized and feeling more powerful than she ever had in her life, Shirley stood and brought up the revolver in front of her. As the figures of Cutbush and the revenant bore down on her one more time, she fired two shots. Both bullets found home, and the figures dissolved and blew apart, holy ash spreading to every corner of the room.

Satisfied that she could do this, Shirley raised her head and arms towards the ceiling and the mass of darkness that was growing there like a cancer. From within the depths of that negative space, she heard, or thought she heard, something roaring and wailing in fear as it tried to muster a response to protect itself. A gigantic head appeared, a mix of Thomas Hayne Cutbush and a dragon with horns curving forth from its skull and flames escaping its nostrils. It roared menacingly as arms and wings formed behind it.

Shirley fired two shots into it.

The first bullet hit the dragon-Cutbush monster, which dissolved in a flash of light. The second flew into the depths of the darkness, leaving a tiny pinprick of white light where it had entered. A moment later, the dark mass of negative space roared and writhed as if it were in pain. It bubbled and expanded, filling up the entire ceiling, before exploding like a hot air balloon. Some of the darkness retreated back into the top of Console Seven and out of sight, while the rest of it caught fire that blazed briefly before dying out.

Shirley sighed and threw the spent revolver away. She did not devote any time to celebrating her victory. Now was not the time to. Now she had to take care of the next big task, which was to—

The Eden Engine rumbled.

Glancing quickly around her, Shirley checked the gauges and saw something was wrong. Two uses of pure energy in a row, the explosion at Console Seven, the death or defeat of the Pure Terror. Any or all of it had overloaded the Engine. And she had a fairly good idea of what was going to happen now that the Engine was overloaded.

Running across the laboratory, she searched and found Griffin, lying unconscious under the remains of the worktable. With a mighty scream, she grabbed hold of a leg and pulled it off him. Whereas before it had been too heavy for her, now it was as light as a basket of sheets for the laundress. Throwing the broken table away, she bent down, tossed Griffin over her shoulder like a burlap sack, and ran out of the laboratory. She had barely time to pause and readjust to the change of light in the hallway before she turned and leapt through the window, crashing through it like a cannonball.

Landing on the grass with catlike grace, Shirley continued running. When she was several meters away from the Lodge, she glanced back behind her. She was just in time to see the north end explode.

An invisible hand composed of heat lifted her off the ground and sent her flying several meters across the lawn. When she hit the ground again, she somehow managed to keep from falling over and instead continued sprinting, putting as much distance between her and the Lodge as possible. Stealing another glance behind her, she saw a great, white light rising into the air before dissipating, leaving behind only flames and smoke, which quickly proceeded to spread along the north wing of the Lodge.

After a while, Shirley noticed how exhausted she was and how heavy Griffin was becoming. Whatever had given her strength and kept her running was leaving her now. Panting, she stopped by an old oak tree, laid Griffin against its trunk, and sat down beside him to watch the distant conflagration consume the Hunting Lodge, lighting up the night with its fury.

Night. When did it become night? So much had happened in the course of the day, she had completely lost sense of time. But that was fine with her. She was happy it was night. Night was the close of day, and she wanted to put a close on this whole experience.

From far away, she could hear the church bell in the Closer Village tolling, alerting the villagers to the fire. Good. Let them deal with it. She was too tired.

From beside her came a groan. Griffin opened his eyes and looked around him in confusion. "Where are we?" Then he started. "The Pure Terror! The Eden Engine! We have to—argh!"

Griffin had tried to stand, only to fall back with a cry of pain. "Something's wrong. I can't move my legs."

"Just rest for now," she said, placing a hand on his shoulder. "I stopped the Pure Terror. The Engine's destroyed."

"It is?" he asked. "What about my uncle?" When Shirley did not answer him, he said, "I see." Then, "Hey, your eye!"

Shirley's hand shot straight to her eye, even though she knew she would not be able to feel any difference. "Is it changed? I had so much pure energy in and around me—!"

"No, no, it's fine." Griffin assured her. "It's the same as before." He cupped her cheek with his hand. "It's perfect."

He leaned towards her. Relieved, Shirley leaned towards him as well, ready to throw practically to the wind for once.

Suddenly something small and white hopped into Shirley's lap. She cried out, startled, only to calm down as she recognized the tiny creature that had found them. "Albedo!"

Albedo mewed and rubbed her head against Shirley's hand. Shirley smiled and laughed. In all the insanity since Nellie had died, she had somehow forgotten about the cat she had adopted. And now, after all that had happened, the one good thing the Eden Engine had produced had made its way back to her.

Scratching behind Albedo's ears, Shirley leaned against Griffin's shoulder, beyond tired. He wrapped his arm around her and said, "What happened after I fell unconscious?"

"Just give me a few minutes," she said. "I'll tell you all about it. But first, let me rest a little while."

So, they rested, and watched as the Lodge burned to the ground.

Chapter Eighteen

Summer, 1895

London, England

There was a knock on the door. "Come in!" Shirley called.

The door opened and Arlene, one of the maids, stepped in. "Excuse me, my lady, but the architects are here."

My lady. She did not think that would ever stop sounding foreign to her ears. It was strange to think that she had a title now, let alone a title that she would have to answer to for the rest of her life.

"Thank you, Arlene," she said. Lifting herself out of her office chair, Shirley walked slowly to the door. She then left her office for Griffin's down the hall. She tried to enjoy moving on her own while she could. Her belly was not noticeable now, but soon it would be, and when it was, she would not be able to do anything but lie in bed all day and wait for the baby to arrive.

She hoped it was a girl. She wanted to name it Lucinda Eleanor Avondale, after the two dear friends she had loved and lost last year.

***

A lot had occurred after the Hunting Lodge had burned down, the first being that Griffin could no longer move his legs and needed a rolling chair to get around. The second, occurring in the Closer Village about a week after the fire and while Griffin was trying to get used to being chair-bound for the rest of his life, had been less upsetting and just as life-changing.

While Griffin had been pushing himself in his chair through the village square to get used to it, and Shirley had watched on in case anything happened to him, a man in a suit and bowler hat had approached them. The man, a barrister named Mr. Neville Castle, introduced himself as the late Sir Joseph's attorney and had come to them to discuss the late baronet's will. When asked why the both of them, and not just Griffin, were needed, Mr. Castle had said, "Because he has named you both as his heirs. And you, Ms. Dobbins, have been named his natural heir."

What followed in the back room of the village's inn had left both Shirley and Griffin's minds reeling. According to Mr. Castle, Sir Joseph had become convinced that Shirley was his daughter by blood much earlier than Shirley had realized, before even the first live experiments with the Engine. Thus convinced, he had taken steps to ensure that she would be taken care of in case of his demise. Normally, England's bastardy laws would have prevented her from inheriting any property. Thus, the Hunting Lodge, all the surrounding property, and all finances and holdings in the baronet's name would have passed to Griffin, Sir Joseph's only remaining legitimate relative. A total of a million pounds in land, cash and stocks were at stake, more than Shirley had ever thought to make in a lifetime.

"However, I was able to find some loopholes to the laws," Mr. Castle had explained, "and so long as Mr. Avondale signs a notarized document that he will not contest the will, and you sign a document stating you are Sir Joseph's natural daughter, you can still inherit the property."

"I do not plan to contest the will," Griffin had quickly stated. "I will sign whatever you want me to."

Mr. Castle nodded. "And you, Miss Dobbins?"

Shirley had thought about it for a minute. Finally, she sighed and said, "It's possible Sir Joseph was my father. I know he was going into London at the time my mother would have gotten pregnant. She never said who my father was. And he did say he had found something out right before he...right before he died. At the very least, I know he thought of me as his daughter. And...and I would be lying if I said I did not feel as if he were a father to me."

In the end, they had both signed the papers. And like that, Shirley Dobbins, who had grown up dirt poor in the slums of Whitechapel and Spitalfields with an alcoholic mother and had worked as a maid with the goal of someday becoming a head housekeeper, had inherited a million pounds in land, cash and stocks. She would never have to work again. Not unless she wanted to, anyway.

Mr. Castle had pocketed the papers in his briefcase and had then said, "As for the title of the Baronet of Hunting, Sir Joseph intended for that title to go to you, Mr. Avondale."

Griffin was surprised. As far as he had known, his uncle had not cared for him at all. His uncle had, in fact, tried to kill him during the height of his madness. To think he had been given anything in Sir Joseph's will, let alone the title of baronet, must have been quite the shock. "He did?"

Mr. Castle had nodded. "Provided, of course, some minor caveats: you have to marry Ms. Dobbins, and you have to sign a prenuptial agreement stating you will not lay claim to Ms. Dobbins' fortune or property after you are married. And you must be married within a year of Sir Joseph's death."

That decision had required a bit more discussion. But after twenty minutes alone, Shirley had called for Mr. Castle to return to the back room for their decision.

A week later, Griffin and Shirley were married in the Closer Village's church. And thus Mr. Griffin Avondale became Sir Griffin Avondale, Baronet of Hunting, and Shirley Dobbins became Lady Shirley Avondale, wife of the Baronet of Hunting.

Despite her many reservations, Shirley found that married life was not so bad. Granted, having money to attend to all her and her husband's needs helped. But beyond that, life bound to another person could be quite pleasant. She and Griffin had a good relationship, they kept out of each other's space when one or the other needed it, and, although Shirley did most of the work due to Griffin's injuries, their marital relations were more than satisfactory.

And at night, when the nightmares came to them and made sleep uneasy, they took what comfort they could in each other's arms. For that, above all else, Shirley was grateful. If she had to be married to anyone, she was glad it was someone who not only understood what horrors flitted through her mind, but shared them as well. It wasn't much, but it meant the world to her. Especially on the worst nights.

Not to say that their life was entirely without problems. For one thing, Sir Joseph's will had stated that Shirley and Griffin had to live in the Hunting Lodge at least six months out of the year. Which was difficult due to the Hunting Lodge having burned down, but the language of the will had stated that if the building were to become so badly damaged that a new one should be built, one should be built with all due haste.

So, Shirley had bought a townhouse in London for them, had hired a staff and a team of architects, and had plans drawn up for a new building. Not just newly built, but new. New layout, new architectural styles, new everything. It would be a home for them, one without the taint of the Eden Engine or the Pure Terror lying about it. They might even build the Lodge in a new spot on the estate grounds, if the surveyors felt that was more beneficial than the original spot.

As long as it was new and different, Shirley would be satisfied. Already not a day went by that she didn't think about those she'd lost at the Lodge. She could not go into a kitchen without thinking of Nellie, who would have someday been a great chef herself. She could not change in and out of her fine new clothes without thinking of Lucinda, who had once helped her change out of soiled clothes, and with whom Shirley wished she could have gotten to know better as a friend.

And, of course, she could not look at a science tome or think about the innovations being made everyday without thinking of Sir

Joseph. Every day, she thought of him, how he had gone from just another employer to her employer and teacher, and then had become something of a father figure to her. Now, he was her father. Legally speaking, anyway. She was still unsure if Sir Joseph was her real father. All she had to go on was his insistence that he was, and that might have only been the ravings of a man driven mad by the Pure Terror.

Regardless, she hoped he was. Because while Sir Joseph had brought her a lot of heartbreak, he had also opened her world and given her so much as well. If he was her father, then what he had given her was all the more special. And when their new home was completed, she would be sure to put up a portrait of Sir Joseph somewhere in the building. Just to remind her of all she'd gone through and all she had gained because of him.

***

Later that evening, as they sat reading in their bed on the ground floor, Griffin put his book down and said, "Have you decided which company you would like to invest in?"

Shirley shrugged and saved her place in the science journal she had been reading.

"Not yet," she said, scratching Albedo's ears. The cat, now much bigger than she had been a year ago, enjoyed snuggling between Shirley and Griffin when they lay in bed. Unless, of course, they were having marital relations, in which case she would retire to her bed in the corner of the room and remain there for the night. "I know there are plenty of science-related companies and institutions I could choose from. And they all look promising. But deciding which one to invest in is proving difficult. Especially since there is no way to tell which one will last more than a year. And some of these so-called 'brilliant men' think because I'm a woman and I have a lazy eye that I'm either an idiot or easy to flatter."

Since they had moved into their London residence, Shirley had been looking for something to occupy her attention and pour her energy into. After having been a maid and a laboratory assistant, retiring into the boring routines of what was considered a "proper" British wife sounded boring. And as she had the funding and the freedom to pursue her own interests, she decided she would.

Unfortunately, she doubted anyone anywhere would hire her as a laboratory assistant, even if they did believe she had worked for Sir Joseph on cutting edge sciences and technologies. And now that she was a baronet's wife, becoming a maid was out of the question. But, from reading financial journals, Shirley had found a new interest: business. And as she was learning, she might have a hidden knack for that as well.

Thus, she was seeking to invest in businesses researching and utilizing the latest advances in science and technology. Though as she had stated to Griffin, finding the right business had proven difficult.

"Nobody ever said intelligent men and women cannot be fools," Griffin replied. "But I'm sure you'll find one that meets what you're looking for eventually. And when you do, the science and business worlds will not know the tidal wave that hit them."

Shirley smiled. "Thank you. How has the new drill business been?"

Griffin had decided, soon after their wedding, that he had no intention of living a life of leisure, even if Shirley was willing to let him live that life. Instead, with a wedding gift of ten-thousand pounds, he had set about founding a drill company. His hope was to build his new company up so that it would one day rival the one his father had founded.

"Though I'll be happy if it is just successful," Griffin had admitted to Shirley when he had proposed the idea to her. "After all I've lost in this life, I could live with that." The look that had passed over his face when he had said that had been so forlorn, Shirley had spent a good amount of the day, as well as the night, comforting him.

"Well, I've finally found a site to build the facilities on," he said. "According to Mr. Leopold, my father's old board is terrified of the sort of company the new Baronet of Hunting is planning to set up, and are trying to put pressure where they can to keep me from purchasing the lot. Which, of course, only makes me want to try harder."

"You seem to enjoy the idea that they fear you," Shirley observed.

Griffin shrugged. "Not really. In truth, I hate the idea that they fear me. After everything we've been through, I would hate to be anyone's object of terror. But I enjoy the challenge of outsmarting them. It's like a chess game, though I am no good at chess."

Shirley laughed. "Is that why you won't let me play chess with you? Because you're terrible at it?"

"Well, after you beat Mr. Leopold on your first try, and then on the next three games, why would I want to embarrass myself?"

Shirley and Griffin laughed together, and then they kissed. As they pulled apart, Griffin said the three words Shirley had heard from him so many times: "I love you."

Shirley replied with the three words she had only recently gotten used to saying: "I love you."

What followed next sent Albedo to her bed in the corner. Later, as they lay spooned in bed, Griffin's head resting in the groove where her neck met her shoulder and his hands on her growing belly, his breath soft and slow with sleep, Shirley watched the dying embers in the fireplace. She wanted to make sure none of the ash would come to life and form into the figure of Cutbush or anything else that terrified her.

Only when the embers had died and nothing appeared before her did she finally allow herself to sleep.

April 11th – May 31st, 2020

Acknowledgements

There are so many people I need to thank for this novel being in print today. I may have written the original story, but a novel making it into a reader's hands is never a solo operation. At least, not usually.

Firstly, thanks to the many writers and teachers who helped me research the Victorian era and bring it to life: Karen Foy, author *of Life in the Victorian Kitchen*; Therese O'Neill, author of both *Ungovernable* and *Unmentionable*; Judith Flanders, author of *Inside the Victorian Home*; Ruth Goodman, author of *How to Be a Victorian*; Donald Rumbelow, author of *The Complete Jack the Ripper*; Hallie Rubenhold, author of *The Five*; Stephen Fry and Audible's podcast *Stephen Fry's Victorian Secrets*; and Patrick N. Allitt and The Great Courses' *Victorian Britain* lecture series.

Not to mention the many works of Victorian literature I read to get my mind in the right place for this book and their authors: *Dracula* by Bram Stoker; *Frankenstein* by Mary Shelley; *The Turn of the Screw* by Henry James; *The Strange Case of Dr. Jekyll and Mr. Hyde* by Robert Louis Stevenson; and the *Sherlock Holmes* stories by Sir Arthur Conan Doyle. Plus, the manga *Emma* by Kaoru Mori, which first introduced me to and enchanted me with the Victorian era. Without that series, *The Pure World Comes* might never be written.

Thank you to Ruth Ann Nordin, Timothy Purvis, and Angela Misri. You all took an early look at the novel and gave great feedback to get it in shape for submission. I appreciate that.

Thank you to Danielle Kaheaku and the team at VitaleTek Inc, who first published the story on the Readict story app (and to Patrick Freivald, who introduced me to Danielle and the Readict app in the first place). Thank you to my uncle, Arthur Siegal, Lauren Willens, and the team at Jaffe Law, for looking out for my best interests.

Thank you to the team at Rooster Republic Press. Your cover designs are always top notch, and this one is no exception. I'm so happy that it'll be on bookshelves very soon. Thank you to the Greater Columbus Arts Council, whose grant helped pay for the cover art of this book. Thanks to the many people who read *TPWC* on the Readict app and praised it enthusiastically (one, Iseult Murphy, lent her blurb to the cover, and that deserves its very own thank you).

Thank you to the Overseeing Intelligence I believe runs this crazy universe, and whom I identify through my own personal faith as Hashem. You make so many things possible, and I always appreciate it.

And finally, thank you, Follower of Fear, for reading this book to completion. I hope you had a great time with Shirley Dobbins and seeing her go through her own transformation at the Hunting Lodge. If you like what you read, let me know somehow what you thought, and make sure to tell others as well.

That's all for now. Until next time, my Followers of Fear, good night and pleasant nightmares.

Rami Ungar
April 19, 2022

About the Author

Rami Ungar is an author from Columbus, Ohio specializing in horror and dark fantasy. He is constantly working on new projects and trying to find new ways to scare his readers, the Followers of Fear. In the past, he has self-published two books, *The Quiet Game: Five Tales to Chill Your Bones* and *Snake*, and published the novel *Rose* with Castrum Press. His next book, *Hannah and Other Stories*, will be published with BSC Publishing Group.

When not writing, Rami enjoys reading, following his many interests, and giving his readers the impression that he's not entirely human.

Read more at https://ramiungarthewriter.com/.

CPSIA information can be obtained
at www.ICGtesting.com
Printed in the USA
BVHW081359240922
647552BV00002B/136